REPLICA
REPLICA

REGINA BARTLEY

Dedication

This book is dedicated to Micalea, because she is my soul sister and I don't know what I'd do without her.

#BestFriendsForever

REPLICA

Cover Design and Photography by: Emily Wittig Designs & Photography

It is not in the stars to hold our destiny but in ourselves.

-William Shakespeare

Other Books by Regina Bartley:

The Unbroken Series:

Escaping Heartbreak

Causing Heartbreak

Lasting Heartbreak

The Rosen Brother's Series:

Klay

A home for Caroline

Kory

Standalones:

Moonshine

I am free

15 years to Life

Dirty Nails

<u>REPLICA</u>

REGINA BARTLEY

REPLICA

PROLOGUE

There was a party, a we-are-graduating party at Amber Gold's house. The night was warm, and there was a thick smell of bonfire in the air. Amber was head cheerleader, and it was a senior's only event, which meant anyone who was anyone would be attending. My sister Elise however, wasn't "anyone," far from it actually. She was at home preparing her valedictorian speech, and shopping online for the perfect comforter set for her new dorm room. It was typical weekend behavior for her. I on the other hand, was living life to the fullest and partying my butt off with the rest of the senior class. I mean you're only a senior once right? We were preparing for the real world with red solo cups and a splash of vodka.

I personally despised every person at the party, but with a little liquor they were growing on me.

The fun was just beginning at Amber's house when things took a turn for the worse. Bobby was flipped upside down over a keg when someone yelled, "COPS!" The sirens were growing louder and people were running like their feet were on fire. Trashing my cup on the ground, I snuck around the back of Amber's house and hurried through the thick brush covering the ground. I could feel it scratching against my ankles.   The farther I ran the darker it was. I could no longer see the back porch light from where I stood, only the small white beam cast by the moon. I perched behind an old tree and pulled out my cell phone. Thankfully, I had some battery left because I knew for certain that I was too damn chicken to walk home. I called Elise to come and pick me up, and she answered on the second ring. She fussed, but agreed. She was always there for me when I needed her. No matter what the circumstances or how badly she wanted to say no. She never would.

I told her to pull a couple of houses down from Amber's, and figured she'd be mad the moment I opened the passenger door. I should've known better. She was never mad at me. She loved me, despite my many flaws, and boy did I have many.

Her eyes were caring when she looked at me. She offered a small smile before turning the stereo up and completely lightening the mood. We loved to sing along, although neither one of us could carry a tune. Elise was my best friend even though we couldn't have been more different. We may have looked exactly alike, but our personalities were night and day. No matter, she was still the cream filling to my Oreo, the sweetness to my roughness.

Her laughter filled the inside of the car as we pulled out onto the street.

We were rocking out to Pink and singing at the top of our lungs when a set of headlights appeared directly in front of us. I didn't know what was going on because it all happened so fast. I heard a scream, a screech, and a sonic boom when the collision happened.

Then I woke up.

Eighteen days, eleven hours, and twenty-seven minutes is how long I spent in the hospital after the accident. I had two surgeries on my arm, three broken ribs, and forty-eight stitches in my head, lost all the hearing in my right ear, and some of the hearing in my left, but I was alive. "By some miracle, you survived the accident," was what they'd said. It wasn't a miracle. It was a travesty. They waited until my sister was buried six feet into the ground before telling me that she didn't make it. I missed her funeral. I missed saying goodbye one last time, and I missed watching them lower her into the ground. Why they didn't tell me, I'll never know. What I did know was that I felt like a shell of myself. I felt like half of my heart was taken with my sister when she left this world, and the other half that lay deep in my chest was shattered beyond repair.

Every time I looked in the mirror I saw her face. Her haunting green eyes paralyzed me. Though I knew it wasn't her, it was still petrifying. It terrified me because I was an exact replica of her. Identical twins we were, right down to our toes. In our minds we were different, but on the outside, you couldn't tell us apart. The mirror was my worst enemy now, and I could barely face that reflection.

How could I go on living my life, when every part of my soul felt empty? It may sound crazy to you, but I should have been the one to die in that crash.

1

England

It had been exactly five months since my sister Elise had died. Since it happened, my parents had barely been able to stand the sight of me. I suppose I reminded them of her when they looked at me. We did share the same face after all. They weren't mean to me, at least not with their words, but they'd never look me in the face. They were having a difficult time dealing with her loss, but they acted like they were the only ones hurting, like I hadn't just lost my best friend and my sister. My parents failed to realize how much I was hurting too. So many nights I'd lie in bed and ask why she was the one that was taken from this earth.

8

She was good and pure. She was innocent. Elise was smart, and kind, and all of the things that I wasn't. She was the sweet sister, the one that everyone wanted to be around. She was smart too. She literally had it all. No one liked me, and that was the way that I liked it. I was the one that always got into trouble, and the one who defied my parents every chance I got. I'd show up to parties where I wasn't welcome, and lie to my parent's about it. I couldn't tell you how many times I told them I was studying with friends or shopping. They should've known I was lying. I didn't study or shop. Elise would always try to stop me, but I never listened. I was a hellion and I liked it that way. Well, I used to.

I cuffed my hands over my ears when I heard my Mom's voice calling me from downstairs. The hearing aids made everything twice as loud, and I couldn't stand it. A lot of times I didn't want to wear them for that reason, but it would make my Mom mad because I couldn't hear her when she spoke. Like I needed more reasons to make her hate me.

9

I crawled out of the bed and made my way to the door. "Yeah," I yelled back, cringing at the sound of my own voice.

"I'm heading out. I don't know what time I'll be home." She said. Obviously, she was going to bury herself under a pile of work. It was the only way she knew how to deal with the pain. Hours at the office would turn into days. She was avoiding her problems, and avoiding me.

"Okay," I replied, and listened as the front door slammed closed. A loud jarring rang throughout the house, and I expected pictures to go tumbling to the ground and break, but it never happened. There was barely a single photograph that hung on our dingy walls anymore. Not since the accident. The last thing this family wanted was a reminder of what was lost.

I closed my bedroom door once she was gone, and blew out a pent-up breath. I waited until enough time had passed and I knew she wasn't coming back before I slid the hearing aids from my ears and laid them back on the nightstand. They were so bothersome. I'd rather not hear at all than wear those God-forsaken things.

Looking around my room, it seemed so bare. Before the accident, my room was filled with photos of my sister and me. There were so many memories that hung on my walls. Good memories that I used to want to cherish forever.

Not now.

Now there wasn't a single memory of her in the entire house, except for maybe in her room. My body shivered at the thought of her bedroom. I never wanted to step foot in there again, if I could help it. Just thinking about it was like nails on a chalkboard. It made me wince.

I removed every photograph from my wall, every sentimental thing that reminded me of her. I even took down the mirrors from my room, because I didn't want to scare myself as I walked by them. You can't even begin to imagine what it feels like to see a dead person every time you look in the mirror.

The two of us would've been nineteen on December 8th.

Would've been...

Now I'd be the only one growing older. She'd be stuck at eighteen forever.

With the 8th only three weeks away, I could feel my anxiety tripling to new heights. It would be the first birthday that I would spend without her, and another damn day that I would be trapped inside my horrible thoughts wishing she were with me.

We were only two weeks from graduating high school when she died, and we were supposed to be in college now.

Together.

My eyes filled with tears at the thought. It was her dream, not mine, and she was going to miss out on it because she picked me up from a stupid fucking party.

She probably would've wanted me to go off to college. Hell, I know she would've. I could hear her voice in my head telling me, "college will be the best years of your life."

Yeah, right! I rolled my eyes.

Instead, I was hidden away inside this house, inside my room, and I never wanted to leave. A few times Mom had told me that I needed to get out of the house, but I didn't know if it was for my sake or for hers. She gave up asking after a while when I never agreed. What she didn't know was that I'd been sneaking out my window almost every night. I didn't go far. I would stand at the edge of the fence that connected our property to the neighbors.

I always waited until both my parents were asleep, which was usually very late, before I climbed down the trellis directly outside of my bedroom window. I'd been using it for many years, so I figured any day now that it would give way and send me tumbling to the ground. Probably wasn't my wisest idea after all the rehab with my hand, but I didn't care. Big deal if it injured me. A little pain never hurt anyone.

Inside a divot in the wood fence was where I stuffed my pack of cigarettes and a little orange lighter. It was the only reason that I came outside at all. I never really smoked too much. I mainly did it because it used to annoy my sister.

Our dad was a heavy smoker though. He'd never miss a stolen pack from his carton. He kept me in full supply. I didn't know if my parents had any idea I was smoking. If they did, they never said anything. I was eighteen so technically they couldn't. I was legally old enough to buy cigarettes, if I had enough gumption to go to the store. A few months ago I would have, but now...

Wasn't going to happen...

Besides, if they knew about my smoking, they wouldn't actually fuss or bring it up. That would require talking (a skill they no longer possessed.)

They were good parents for the most part, except now, after the accident. Now I rarely spoke to them. I'd been waiting for the day when they decided to tell me to move out, but it hadn't come yet. Maybe they felt sorry for me.

I inhaled deeply and let my lungs fill up with smoke before exhaling softly. I loved the way it felt when I smoked now. My chest no longer burned. It was more like a euphoric feeling. Like I needed the smoke in my lungs to breathe easier. Weird I know.

I was officially addicted.

"One step closer to killing yourself," would be what my sister would say, if she were there. But she wasn't.

She was never going to be there again.

I sat down in the tall grass next to the fence and flipped open my phone. Just because I wasn't an active member of society, didn't mean that I still didn't like to know what was going on.

I clicked on the Facebook app, and scrolled through the feed. Surprisingly, I had over three hundred friends. It was thanks to my sister, and not me. Or maybe it was because people just liked to be as nosey as I was. They were probably snooping, even though they wouldn't find anything. I never posted. I didn't want people to be all up in my business. The fact that they posted every single stupid thing that they did in their life was on them. They were just asking to be the subject of gossip around town.

Just like every other night, Facebook was a downer, unless you considered baby pictures and vague posting exciting. Maybe that's your thing. It certainly wasn't mine.

Garbage... Scroll...

Bitch... Scroll...

"What the fuck is that..." Scroll...

Yuck... Scroll...

Oh wait... "I know who she's talking about..." Scroll...

Again, there was nothing exciting on Facebook.

It took months for people to stop posting pictures and things about my sister. I couldn't be happier that it had dwindled down to almost non-existent. I couldn't bear to look at them for another minute. It was bad enough that our rooms adjoined with a bathroom, that I now could barely use. I was avoiding my own face, and I sure as hell didn't want to see hers. My parents thought it would be best to leave her room, just as it was. This coming from the parent who thought it was best to never speak or mention her name. Therapists would pay big money to spend a day in our house.

I continued to scroll down the page hoping to catch something interesting, but I wasn't having much luck. It was the same boring things day in and day out.

My phone vibrated, causing me to jump a little, and a little red number one popped up in my messenger box. Someone was messaging me on Facebook.

I hesitated at first, before I opened it.

It was from my neighbor, Will Edmunds.

-That's the third night this week. You know smoking will kill you?

I glanced over my shoulder to see his silhouette in a window at the side of the house. Was he spying on me? And why was he even home? He left town three years ago for school or Army or something. He was only around on the holidays. He shouldn't have been home.

I stared at the screen once more. *Get a life you asshole.* Instead of responding, I held up two middle fingers high in the air. I wasn't completely sure that he could see me clearly enough to know that I was flipping him off, but I was hoping.

My phone buzzed again.

-Is that an invitation?

Yeah right. I thought to myself. I wasn't about to give him the satisfaction of a response, so hopefully he'd take the hint. I didn't want to talk. Not to anyone.

-I was kidding.

And I was over *this*. Whatever the hell "this" was.

I hid my cigarettes back in their spot and walked back over to the trellis that I had climbed down from. I didn't look back at his house. Maybe I wanted to, but I didn't. It only took me a second to climb back up. I probably could've used the front door.

I mean my parents didn't care what I did or when I did it. It was just in my nature to do something secretive. I wasn't ready to try picking a fight with my parents, although they probably wouldn't even notice.

Once I was safely inside, I peeked out my bedroom window and across the yard to Will's house. The light that was once on was now off. Thank goodness. We hardly knew each other even though we'd lived next to each other for over ten years. There had never even been an instance where we had spoken. He was a few years older, and never home. Why he would want to talk to me now was unbeknownst to me.

Maybe he thought I was my sister.

I shivered.

Surely, he knew that I wasn't.

She never spoke to him either.

I let the navy blue curtain fall back down to block the outside world once again. My room was dark except for the light coming from the small television in the corner.

I didn't bother changing. Instead, I just kicked off my shoes and crawled into bed. I'd made it through another day without her, and I'm not sure how. This one seemed like the longest one yet, but I'm sure tomorrow would feel longer.

I reached into a drawer in my nightstand and grabbed my bottle of sleeping aids that I asked my Mom to pick up from the store. They weren't working too well, but it was my only hope for getting any sleep at all. I couldn't believe that she even bought them for me. All I did was write down "something to help me sleep" on the list that hung on the fridge. A couple of days later they were in my bathroom on the counter.

My ghostly mother wouldn't even walk into my room to give them to me. She left them on the counter. Guess I couldn't blame her. I wouldn't want to look at me either. I'm sure that every time she did, she wished that I were Elise.

I swallowed two of the pills and pulled the blanket up tightly around my neck. All I wanted was one restful night's sleep. I wouldn't pray for it though, because I didn't deserve answered prayers. I was given life. I had no reason to ask for anything else.

2

Will

What the hell was I doing messaging her?

The screams came from down the hall in Dad's bedroom, and suddenly I knew exactly what I was doing.

ESCAPING.

She was right there in my sights, close enough that I could skip a rock and hit her. Not that I would do that, but she stood there in the dark just feet away nearly every night, and I wanted to be there with her. Years of being neighbors and I'd never once talked to her.

This was different. The timing was different. We had a connected past. She wasn't aware of it, but I was. She had no idea that we shared more than just a fence.

I let myself fall back onto the bed and closed my eyes.

After my Mom died I came back here hoping that staying with my Dad and Stepmom would help ease my thoughts, maybe take my mind off of the accident. I'd forgotten about the constant fighting, or maybe I just hoped that the two of them had finally outgrown it.

Wrong.

They were still going strong. They loved it. They loved the screaming, the crunching sounds that their fists made against the drywall, and the way it felt to have their hands wrapped around the other's neck. It was no wonder I fucking left this place. My Mom was nothing like that. She was sweet, and kind. She left my Dad when I was about nine years old. She hated the fighting too. It wasn't in her nature to argue. She just didn't have it in her, and I couldn't blame her.

I didn't have it either. It made me sick at my stomach just listening to them in the other room.

My Dad never put his hands on me, and wouldn't. Not even as a child did he ever hit me. But the way he and my stepmom fought would make a grown man squirm. They were brutal to each other. I couldn't wait to get my own place and get the hell out of there.

The first couple of months that I was back here, I stayed with my buddy Daniel and sometimes Jace. He was another one of the guys that I grew up with. But Jace's studio was barely big enough to fit his ass in. It was too damn crowded, and though he didn't seem to mind, I just felt too cramped. And Daniel just moved his fiancé Melody in with him, so I felt like I was intruding every time I was there. She was nice and all, but they needed their space. It had grown past time for me to start looking for my own place.

I wasn't even working. I had a job at Mark's Grill downtown, but I showed up late twice last week and he fired me. Too much partying was bad for keeping a job. It didn't take an idiot to know that. I guess I just didn't care that much. What I really wanted was to go back to school.

It was what my Mom would've wanted for me. She was always encouraging me to make something of myself. "Don't be a loser," she'd say. But what she meant was –Don't be your Father.

I couldn't be him.

I wouldn't.

All I wanted was a little time to grieve, a little time to throw caution to the wind. I was about to turn twenty-one, and I wanted one last hoorah before I said goodbye to this fucking place, and left a trail of dust behind me.

Looking back out my bedroom window, I noticed that England's bedroom light was off. She must've gone to sleep.

I envied her.

Sleep didn't come easy for me. I can't remember the last time I'd slept for more than four hours.

I wondered what she thought about in that room all day? Not that I was a stalker.

25

Okay, so maybe I watched her more than I should, but I couldn't help myself. There was something about her that sucked me in. For months she hasn't been out of that house, or at least not that I'd ever seen. She paced in front of her window sometimes. I could see her small reflection through the window blinds when her curtains were pulled back away from her bedroom window. Back and forth, she'd walk, and I'd let myself get lost in her movement. I blamed it in just a way to pass the time, but I might've secretly hoped she'd get undressed so that I could watch.

You couldn't blame a guy for wishing.

I don't know what made me message her tonight, but I felt like I needed to. Like it was my chance to finally speak to her after months of guessing her every move. I thought maybe she needed to decompress as much as me.

Our chat was short and sweet, and she was too much of a firecracker for my lame moves. I blame it on a lack of sleep, because I made a complete ass out of myself and she flipped me off in the process. I never had to do much talking around women. The easier the crowd was, the better. Or maybe I should say the drunker the crowd was, the better.

England was different than the drunken woman I slept with. She obviously belonged on that side, because she most certainly didn't belong on mine. I would never work that hard for a piece of ass anyway.

And some hot chick on top of me was just what I needed to let out my frustrations.

I grabbed my boxers and my jeans off my dresser and took a quick shower before heading out. Jace said there was a party at Robin's house. I knew what that meant. He didn't have to say anything else. I'd have my pick of any girl I wanted for the night.

Well, almost any girl.

Fireball shots, girls, and one helluva time, was just what the doctor ordered.

My tires spun as my Mustang peeled out of the gravel driveway. Robin's house was only ten minutes or so from my house. I knew the place all too well. Her parties were part of the reason for my tardiness at work. Once you got inside, you didn't want to leave.

Pun intended.

3

England

After waking up several times throughout the night, I finally gave up. It was pointless to keep fighting myself for more sleep when it was a never-ending battle that I was losing. Every night it was the same thing time and time again. I'd close my eyes and the medicine would allow me to drift away, but once the nightmares hit or my body reached my four-hour maximum it was all –heads up buttercup- for me. Insomnia was a bitch that had me chained up like a rabid dog.

You'd think that I'd be accustomed to the lack of sleep by this point, but you'd be wrong. It made me irritable, and moody. There were several instances where I could cry at the drop of a hat.

Like now... Just feeling the tiredness seeping through me made me want to lose control and cry out. I wanted to scream, "It's not fair dammit." But I'd shove that feeling back deep inside where it belonged. What was fair anyway?

It's just another day, England.

Glancing over at the door, I knew that no one had come in to check on me. I had strategically placed a pile of dirty clothes up against the back of my door so that I would know. Just like the night before, they hadn't moved. They weren't scooted back. They were still lying in the exact same place I'd put them. They hadn't moved an inch, not one single inch.

Of course, why would they? It was stupid of me to think that my parents cared enough to come check on me. They didn't even do that when Elise was alive. Why would they start now? It was foolish of me to wish for their affections.

I placed my left hearing aid into my ear and winced when the first ringing sound hit me. I didn't bother with the right one, because it barely helped me anyway. As long as I could hear out of one of my ears, it was all I needed.

Opening the door to my bedroom, I made my way down the carpeted steps, and into the kitchen. The house was oddly quiet for six a.m. normally the coffee would be on, and I would at least hear a shower running. There was no movement at all. The only sound I heard was the stupid humming that my hearing aid made with my every movement. I squinted as the morning light shined brightly through the kitchen window. With quiet footsteps, I made my way towards my parent's bedroom. Peeking around the doorframe, I saw that their bed was made. There was no sign of them.

"Must be gone to work," I shrugged.

I made myself a bowl of cereal and went into the family room to watch T.V. There was a note folded up on the coffee table with my name on it. I recognized my mother's writing. I set my bowl down and picked up the paper.

England,

Work is sending me to Cleveland for a conference. I'll be gone until Tuesday. Your father is joining me on the trip. If you need something call my cell or your father's. There is a twenty-dollar bill in the coffee container above the fridge if you need it. Maybe while we are away you can job hunt. Talk to you soon.

Mom

A job? I sneered. We'd never talked about me getting a job before. Of course she would write it in a note, and not tell me to my face.

I wadded the paper up and threw it across the room with as much force as I could. Too bad it wasn't heavy enough to break something.

This trip of hers probably wasn't even work related. They just needed to get away from here, and away from me. I was a walking disease, stay near me too long and you might catch it.

The more I thought about job-hunting, the more it made me sick. I knew the day would come soon enough, and I'd have to venture out into society again, but I wished I could join a whole new society, one that didn't know me and wouldn't look at me differently. I needed a new zip code. There were too many people in this town that knew me, or at least thought that they did anyway.

I removed my hearing aid because I hated that damn thing, and propped my feet up on the coffee table. With my parents gone my hearing aid wasn't necessary. I could listen to the T.V. as loud as I wanted. Shoveling in another bite of my Captain Crunch cereal, I cranked the T.V. to seventy-eight. It was the perfect number for me to hear it plainly. It must've been my lucky day too because my favorite station was having an all day gore marathon. That meant back-to-back scary movies.

Scary movies were my thing; especially the ones that made you check behind closed doors and curtains. Elise used to hate them. If I made her sit with me while I watched them she'd put her earphones in.

She said the music made it much worse because you always knew when something bad was about to happen. The anticipation was killer. After I made her watch *The Cabin in the Woods,* she slept in my bed with me for a week. I vowed never again to make her watch another scary movie. She was the hardest person in the world to sleep with. I'm not exaggerating.

I smiled at the thought of her mouth gaping open and her loud snores.

It was the first time in a while that I'd had good memories of Elise and already the note from my Mother was long forgotten, at least until I had to get off the couch. But I didn't intend on leaving it for the rest of the day if I could help it. All I wanted to do was lie around and be the laziest person ever, lazy with a capital L.

I made myself comfortable with the couch blanket and my Mother's silky throw pillow. A big no-no if she were there, but I wouldn't even be lying on the couch if she were there.

"I'm laying on your precious pillow, Mom!" I yelled out. It was funny how much better I felt when she wasn't home. Her crabby mood kept me in a crabby mood.

Always.

I must've dozed off somewhere in the middle of my fright fest. The last thing I remember was someone's head being chopped off. The graphics from the movie were terrible, so it must've lured me to sleep. They just didn't make scary movies that were worth watching years ago. Over the years, they've gotten much better.

I felt the nudge of someone's hand on my arm, but figured I must've been dreaming. That was until the nudge turned frantic, and it felt like I was being jarred senseless.

My eyes fluttered open, and a shrilling scream escaped my throat. I swung my fist up at his face with force, connecting with his nose as I scrambled falling off the couch. It was a bittersweet crunch under my knuckles that left my hand on fire as I crawled as fast as I could to toward the door, in an escape to leave.

I could have easily been mistaken for one of those bimbos in the horror films. You know, the stupid ones who took too long to run, or tried crawling out a hole they couldn't fit through. Or ran upstairs instead of out the open front door. I paused to turn around.

I paused.

Could we just talk about how stupid that would've been if my killer had been holding a gun?

Luckily for me, it was smart to turn around. I realized then that it was my next-door neighbor Will. He wasn't touching me, although he was just feet away. But his arm was stretched out in front of him and too close for me to feel comfortable.

"I'm sorry, please, I'm so sorry." His mouth moved over and over with the same apology. I could hear nothing but a mumble without my hearing aids. I could only read his lips.

"What the hell are you doing in my house?" I yelled, getting up on my two feet. I must've looked like an idiot down on all fours. Once I was able to see him more clearly, I could tell that I'd nailed his face good.

The blood was running from his nose, and his eyes were tearing up.

He took a step forward, and I jumped back keeping one hand firmly on the doorknob. I needed an easy getaway because if he inched his way any closer I was going to run. No doubt about it.

When his mouth started moving, I could no longer read his lips. They were moving too fast. He was in a rush to tell me whatever it was he needed to tell me, and I couldn't make heads or tails of it.

"Stop!" I yelled. My free hand was locked straight in front of me. I pointed to my ear and shook my head. "I can't hear you." My voice was entirely too loud for our conversation, but I could still hear the television, so I was trying to talk above it.

There was an understanding look on his face, something I wasn't expecting. He held up one finger in a motion for me to hold on, and backed up slowly.

I glared at him, but didn't move.

When he reached the edge of the coffee table, he picked up the remote. The television volume went to nonexistent. I could no longer hear it, which was wise. Maybe then I'd stop yelling. He took a few slow steps back in my direction, cautioning his every move. That made him appear even more like a stalker than he already did, but this time in a funny way. It was like he was scared I might hit him again, and I looked at the floor to keep from laughing.

I startled when his hand stretched out to me. In his palm was my hearing aid, which I'd forgotten I'd left on the table next to the couch. Reaching for it swiftly, I placed it in my ear. The squeal of it made me cringe.

"Okay," I said in a frustrated tone. "Explain now, then get out of my house."

"Can you hear me?" He asked.

"Yes, Sherlock. I can hear you. Now speak."

"I knocked on the door several times, but you didn't answer."

"So you thought you could just walk in and make yourself at home?" My patience was as thin as ice, and he was about to fall through it and freeze to death.

"No, no, that's not it at all. I was about to leave when I heard a horrible scream. I thought something was wrong or that someone was inside trying to kill you. I didn't know. So I came in." He brushed his hand under his nose to wipe the blood away. "I made it to the couch before I realized it was the television. I had to wake you up though, because I burst through the door, and broke it." He pointed at the door, and I looked closely to see the wood chipped away from the top and a bend in the frame. "I'm sorry about that. I'll fix it. I was just worried that something bad was happening, and I didn't know what to do."

"What if my parents had been home? My Dad probably would've shot you." Not really. He didn't even own a gun, but Will didn't need to know that.

"I saw them leave early this morning," he admitted.

"Is there a reason you're stalking me?"

His jaw tightened, "I'm not stalking you. I came over this morning to see if you wanted to go get some breakfast with me, and then you punched me."

39

I smiled, even though I was trying hard not to. "I don't want your breakfast, I want you to leave, and don't come over again. If someone is trying to kill me, oh well. I don't need you running in here like some big, bad, protector."

"I," he started to speak.

"No. Whatever you're about to say, just don't. You can leave now."

"I have to fix your door."

Shit. He was right. I stretched out my neck and stared at the ceiling. My parents would freak if they saw it. Stupid boy.

"Fine," I growled, crossing my arms over my chest. It was the first time I'd realized that I was braless in my tee shirt. Thank goodness he wasn't staring at my chest. I don't think he realized it, or if he did, he didn't let on.

"I'll go get my dad's toolbox." I stomped off.

"England," he stopped me.

"Yeah."

"Would you please get me a rag for my face?" The blood was smeared half over his cheek and his right hand was covered.

I nodded, and left the room, stomping the whole way.

So much for a relaxing morning on my couch, thanks to him. Hopefully, he worked fast because I'd had more than enough human interaction for one day.

Both of Will's eyes were already turning black when I came back with the wet rag. I felt kind of bad. But it was his fault. He shouldn't have come storming into my house as if he owned the place.

"Sit on the step," I told him, pointing to the staircase behind him. He listened quite nicely covering the third step with most of his behind. Standing in front of him, we were eye to eye, which showed just how tall this man was.

"You have a powerful right hook," he said, tilting his head slightly to left.

"Obviously, since your eyes are black," I rebutted. "I wouldn't tell too many people what happened. They'll think you're a pansy if you're getting beat up by a girl."

I gently wiped the blood away from his cheek, trying not to apply too much pressure.

"I'll tell them it was a bar fight with a seven-foot tall man wearing steel-toed boots."

"Good choice," I replied.

Being this close to Will, I could see every line on his face. He had a small dimple on his left cheek, and a plump bottom lip. His eyes were a dark shade of brown, which made them look almost black. Those eyebrows were perfectly shaped, almost too perfect. And that nose, it was perfect despite the fact it was bleeding. It had been a long time since I'd been this close to a guy. He had a scruffy, need-to-shave face, that I let my hand touch gingerly as I wiped the blood away.

What was I doing?

"Here," I tossed the rag to him. "Take a right when you get into the kitchen. The bathroom is the second door on the left."

He gave me a questioning look, then stood up. I moved past him quickly taking the stairs as fast as I could. It probably made me look like an idiot, but I didn't care. I had to remove myself from the situation. It was unsettling in my stomach. I hadn't spoken to anyone since the accident, and there I was acting like a normal girl. The thought terrified me, and all I wanted to do was put on a damn bra, and hide away in my room.

The bra was doable, but I couldn't stay hidden in my room while some stranger was in the house. Maybe he was using me as an excuse to steal us blind. Who knew? Or maybe he thought he could come over and seduce me. What was I saying?

I'd officially gone bananas.

I was going to go back downstairs, take my seat on the couch, and not say another word until he was gone. At least that was my plan.

It sure sounded good.

I slipped a bra on under my PJ's and went back downstairs. I felt him watch me as I made my way back to the couch, but he didn't say anything, and

43

neither did I. Slipping out my hearing aid on purpose, I turned the T.V. back to seventy-eight and went back to watching my horror movies, or so I tried. Knowing he was there made it a whole lot harder for me to concentrate on the movie.

4

Will

I growled under my breath as I watched her sit roughly down on the couch. She turned the television up so loud that I couldn't hear myself think. That blasted television mixed with the pain in my face made me wish I hadn't played knight-in-shinning-armor. I made the stupidest decisions sometimes.

I blinked back the tears that filled my eyes. My nose hurt like a bitch. She hit me good. It felt like my nose was stretched halfway across my face or it had been rearranged and was now sitting upwards between my eyes. Thank goodness there were no mirrors in sight. I'd hate to see what it looked like. I glanced around to be sure that there wasn't a hidden mirror that I hadn't seen, but nothing. In fact, the walls were mostly bare. No photographs, no embarrassing school moments, nothing. It was stale, and plain, not like what you'd expect from a family room. Even our living room was livelier than this one, and it was torn to shreds.

Assessing the damage of the door, I shook my head. Could I have made a bigger ass of myself? Barging in through the door like I owned the place, and coming face to face with her...

It was nothing like I'd pictured it to be. Not that I'd pictured it. It's just that when I came bursting through the door I was ready to save her. I was more than able to protect the girl in need. Only she wasn't needy at all. She had a much rougher exterior than I expected. I thought she'd be shy and timid, or maybe she'd be nice and quiet. I should've known better after she'd given me the finger last night.

She was a beautiful girl but aggravating, and she had a fiery look in her eyes. Did I mention how beautiful she was? She's gorgeous.

When I watched her come down those steps earlier, I thought to myself that I wished she would fall so I could catch her. I wanted any kind of excuse to get my arms around her tiny little waist.

Talk about shit-out-of-luck. She was going to make certain that I kept my distance no matter what, like now, with her sitting on the couch. It was thoroughly annoying the piss out of me. All I could see was the back of her head bobbing around. She was fidgeting like she was having some internal confrontation in her head. I wanted to march over there and pull her hair out of that funky looking ball she had it in. Instead, I just shook my head and wished that I had some earplugs because her annoying television and her annoying head bobbing and, well, she was annoying...

I growled again.

I should've never stopped at the edge of my driveway. I should've kept on going. Of course, that would've been too easy. No. I had to swoop in and save the day. Dammit, why did she have to be so pretty?

Grrr.

She got under my skin.

I felt like an ass for barging in, and an even bigger ass when I scared her half to death. But that girl was tampering on the edge of my nerves. The flipping T.V. wasn't helping.

To think that I almost felt sorry for her when she told me that she couldn't hear me. I hated watching her put that hearing aid in her ear. I knew what caused it. I knew all about the wreck she was in. It totally fucked her up. That was easy to see.

If I was going to be stuck in this house all day with her, then I was going to have to make the best of it. Little did she know I could be just as annoying as she was, maybe even worse?

Glancing back at the door, I realized that I was going to need some different hardware and my Dad's tool belt. Thankfully, I could fix it without replacing the whole door.

"England," I called out to her, but she never moved. "England!" I yelled. She couldn't hear me, or she was choosing not to which was far more logical.

I closed my eyes and tilted my head back silently cursing under my breath.

"Kill me now," I muttered.

Shaking my head, I made the short walk to the couch to get her attention. Silently I thought of a million things that I'd like to do with that T.V., but that would mean a million more things I'd have to fix.

No, thank you!

5

England

Watching scary movies will make you jumpy anyway, and when someone unexpectedly touches you while watching, it's ten times worse. I nearly peed on myself when Will tapped my shoulder to get my attention. My butt must have come off the couch a good six inches. He was lucky that he didn't get knocked out again. Only this time it would've been my fault for taking my hearing aid out.

I gave him a look that could kill over my shoulder before reaching for my hearing aid. I didn't want to hear a damn thing he had to say, and I sure as hell didn't want to talk to him. Clearly, he saw the aggravated look on my face.

"Yeah," I said. I reached for the remote and turned the T.V. down so I wouldn't have to yell above it. I must've looked like an idiot screaming at him earlier, and probably even more ridiculous when he realized I needing my hearing aid.

"I have to go to the hardware store because I don't have all the parts I need."

"Okay." My dull expression spoke volumes, I'm sure.

"Get your shoes on, you're going too."

"No, no I'm not. You broke the door, and you can fix it. Nowhere in my plans does it say I'm to assist you today. You're the one who barged in here and wrecked my perfectly good nap. My entire day of movie watching and laziness is ruined because of you."

"Are you always so bitchy?" He growled.

Oh no, he didn't!

I stood up from my couch and stomped over to stand directly in front of him. Granted I was a mere five foot two, while he stood well over six feet.

"What did you say?" I spat.

"I asked if you were always this bitchy."

I reared back and hit him square in the nose. Again.

This time, he fell right to his knees and moaned. "I can't believe you punched me again." His voice was nothing but a mumble as his hand blocked his mouth. Blood started dripping onto the carpet.

Crap.

I ran to the kitchen to grab a towel from the drawer for his face. My parents would flip if there were bloodstains on the carpet. Why couldn't I keep myself in check? For some reason, he infuriated me. Almost everything he said made me want to claw his eyes out.

Maybe not his eyes, they were too pretty.

That nose though, it'd be as crooked as a politician once I was done with him.

I ran back into the living room where I found him bent over, moaning in pain. My first thought was that I was being such a bitch to him. It was no wonder he said I was bitchy, because I was. But I didn't like hearing him say it. He should keep his big, fat, feelings to himself.

Hearing the way he groaned in pain made me feel a little guilty. I was almost positive that I'd broken his nose this time. There was a nasty crunching sound when my fist connected with it.

"Here," I said, pushing the towel towards his face.

His eyes narrowed in fury. "You're lucky you're not a man," he snarled. "I think I need a doctor. Ow," he cried out in pain when he pressed the towel to his face. He was hurt pretty badly.

This was awful. I'd screwed up royally. "Are your parents home?"

"No. But even if they were you'd still be taking me. Get dressed."

"What? No! I'm not going anywhere."

He reached into the pocket of his faded jeans and without notice, tossed his car keys at me. "Yes, you are."

"Call an ambulance!" I shouted. I hadn't been away from my house in months, much less driven a car. He expected me to take him to the ER. Did he know how much I despised that place? I never wanted to step foot inside that building again. And drive? I couldn't.

I just couldn't.

My hands felt clammy against the rough set of keys. It was too much. There was no way I could do it. My heart was hammering inside my chest just thinking about it.

"I can't do it." I shook my head profusely in a bit of a panic. "I can't."

With his free hand, he reached out and touched my cheek. I didn't shy away, or move at all for that matter. There was a small tinge of relief as his rough calloused hand moved gently against my face. "Stop," he said, and the way he said the word wasn't mean or unjust. It was calm and steady, which was exactly what I needed. "You can do this. You have to do this." The intensity of his words made me question if there were a hidden meaning behind them. I'd punched him in the nose, and he was showing me kindness that I didn't deserve.

Looking clearly at his face I watched the blood from his nose run down his face and drip. The toe of his boots caught it before it could reach the carpet. It looked gruesome. My stomach could hardly take it.

Damn. Damn. Damn.

Why did I punch him in the face?

"Get dressed. Hurry please, before I bleed to death," he grumbled before situating the rag more comfortably at his nose.

I released a heavy breath out of frustration. "Don't joke like that. It's not funny. Go get in the car before I punch you again.

Throwing caution to the wind, I ran upstairs to change my clothes. I grabbed my wallet and cell phone off my dresser. In a brief moment of self-doubt, I nearly called 911 from my cell. It would've been easy to press and hold the nine key on my cell keypad and get an ambulance to come get him instead.

No. You punched him. You take him. You can't stay locked up in this house forever. I thought to myself.

I pulled the front door closed, but didn't bother locking it. It was broken. Hopefully, everything would be inside when I got back.

I scrambled off the porch and towards the driveway. He couldn't have left because I still had his keys. A horn beeped from a distance and then again. He was honking at me from his driveway. I blocked the sun from my eyes with my hand to make sure it was really him, and he honked again. I guess I hadn't thought about him walking over to my place.

I walked swiftly around the edge of the fence that separated our property and stepped onto his yard. His car was parked near the end of their long driveway, just a few yards away from me, so I jogged the rest of the way to his vehicle. This was a hurried matter.

Regina Bartley

Swinging the driver's side door open, I climbed inside the dark blue Mustang. The seat was so far back that I couldn't reach the pedals or the steering wheel.

"Let's go," he urged.

I pulled the lever under the seat and scooted it up so that I was close enough to drive. I put my hand on the wheel, but that was when I froze. Every working part of my body no longer worked. I didn't know what to do with my hands, and even if I did, they wouldn't cooperate. I was scared shitless.

"You do know how to drive right?" He asked.

"Yes, would you shut up for a second." I barked. "I'm trying to have a perfectly good meltdown here, and you're ruining it."

"Jesus, would you look at my face? No more meltdowns okay? I need urgent medical care. Put the key in the hole, turn it, put the car in reverse, and back the hell up out of this driveway."

"Will!" I screamed. "I swear that if you say one more smart word I am going to punch that broken nose of yours clear up into your head." I could feel my blood boiling under my skin. He was making the situation way harder than it needed to be.

I put the key into the ignition and started the car. I was fuming mad.

"You know, you could be a little more sensitive to me since I'm in a shit load of pain right now."

Breathe in. I had to remind myself to breathe. "You want to talk to me about being sensitive. For the past however long you've been at my house, you've been a pain in my ass. I didn't ask for you to come disrupt my life today. Do you think this is what I want to be doing while I have the whole house to myself? Because it's not." I kept up the ranting as I pulled onto the road. "You don't know how hard it is for me to be out in public, and furthermore, you don't know what a struggle it is to be in a car or driving for that matter. You're a real..." I struggled for the right word, "...a real selfish bastard."

"Hey!" He shouted back. "I'm not the one that goes around punching people."

"You deserved it."

"Oh really. Why? Because I said you were bitchy. Well, you are. I wasn't lying."

"Do you see my hands?" I growled. They were gripping the stair wheel with force. "When I stop this car, I'm going to wrap them around your neck."

"Why the violence? Maybe you should see the doctor instead of me." Even the tone of his voice was grating on my nerves.

Thankfully the local emergency room was less than five miles from us, because I was ready to dump his ass at the curb. I pulled into the closest parking spot I could find and put the car into park. I turned it off and tossed the key onto his lap.

"You can see your precious doctor now, you happy?" I let the sarcasm drip freely from my voice.

"Very," he replied with a sexy smile.

That smile pissed me off too.

"You did it. You drove us here, and all I had to do was fight with you."

Well, fuck me! I did do it. I could feel the shock that must've been written all over my face. I huffed in exasperation.

"Thank you England," he said as he leaned over and kissed my cheek.

I was surprised by how easily it was for him to kiss me, and how much I wanted him to do it again. I was surprised that I drove him there without having any more meltdowns. But even more so, I was surprised that he knew just how to handle me and make me overcome my fear.

Good grief, why was he so hot all of a sudden?

"Come on. I need a doctor." He opened the passenger door to climb out.

"Wait. I can't go in there. I hate hospitals."

"You've made it this far, come on. I need you to hold my hand."

I took one look at his pitiful, pouty face, and I gave in.

I gave in.

Maybe I did need to see a doctor.

"Gosh dammit," I grumbled. "Sensitive bastard."

6

Will

I can't believe the puppy-dog face worked on her. She was softening up to me, and according to my watch it was record time. It only took a punch in the face and an awkward fight behind the wheel.

And she was funny, so funny. Who would've guessed that?

I squeezed her hand in mine with a little extra force as we sat in the waiting area of the E.R. I wanted her to think that I was in much more pain than I really was. Don't get me wrong -there was pain- but I couldn't help myself for laying on a little guilt trip, you know?

Plus, I'd planned on keeping our hands locked as long as I could get away with it.

The hospital clearly made her uncomfortable. I could tell by the way she slumped over when she walked from the moment we entered through the double doors, and the faces she made as she looked around the room. She'd wince every time someone in a hospital gown came into view.

Despite her bitterness and hard shell, I knew she could overcome her fears. I saw her do it firsthand when she drove my car. Though she constantly drove me crazy, I couldn't deny that I wanted to be close to her in every single way possible. It was completely out of the ordinary for me.

But she was completely unordinary.

As we sat there in the waiting room with our hands locked together, I could feel my hand starting to sweat. I never let go though. The moment that I released her hand would be the exact time that she'd bolt out the doors at ninety miles per hour.

We sat in silence for at least forty minutes before my name was called.

Her ass must've been glued to the chair, because I felt like I had to lift her with a crane out of it. She pulled back on my hand without saying a word, and I knew that it was a plea for me to let her go, but I wasn't about to.

Instead, I gently rubbed my thumb over the top of her hand and with a slight tug; I pulled her along with me. Inside the small room, she stood next to me as the nurse asked a series of uncomfortable question. Not really uncomfortable to me, but clearly to England. She kept her eyes on the floor and her back slumped over. If the nurse didn't know any better she'd think that England was mute. Aside from her breathing, she never said a word.

"We need to take you down for x-rays," the nurse said.

I looked over at England, and she glared at me with the evilest eyes. I knew right then that the puppy-dog face wouldn't work this time.

"You have any handcuffs?" I asked the nurse. Obviously, it was a one-sided joke because the nurse had steam coming out of her ears. It wasn't my finest

63

moment, but I didn't want England disappearing on me.

"Don't leave," I whispered to her.

Her eyes glanced behind me, but never landed on my face.

"Please don't leave," I whispered again.

She could loosen the damn leash around my neck. I was choking on my own words, and gagging on my balls.

I was only one step away from getting down on all fours and licking my own ass.

"For the love of God Woman! You broke my nose."

I could see inside her fiery eyes that she was about to break it again.

"Let's go," the nurse said.

"Don't leave," I said one more time before getting off the bed.

"I WON'T!" She growled through her teeth.

I grinned at her before the nurse led me from the room because I knew it would make her angrier.

And if there was thing I was good at, it was provoking the beast.

7

England

Four grueling hours, that's how long it took to learn that his nose was broken.

I broke it.

Yep, it was me.

I sort of felt like a boss, like I owned that shit. It was my first fight, well one-sided fight nonetheless, but I kicked ass. I wouldn't have been bragging, but the doctor said he didn't need surgery. So in other words, I could brag all I wanted. With a little pain medicine and an ice pack, he'd be good as new. In a week or so.

"Can you take me home now?" I grumbled, stretching my arms wide over my head. Spreading my wings was exhausting. It was far too much for one person to endure in one day. I'd driven, I'd gone inside the hospital, and I'd had human interaction. I couldn't take anymore.

"Sure, I need someone to take care of me the rest of the day," he replied. His voice was a bit nasally from the bandaging. It was kind of cute, in an annoying sort of way.

"You have a mother, and I have a couch calling my name."

His eyes searched my face.

For what, I didn't know.

I had no plans in begging for an apology. The only thing on my mind was getting home. I wanted to be back in my comfort zone as quickly as possible. He had no idea the courage it took for me to do what I'd done today.

No idea.

Even without realization the entire situation freaked me the hell out.

"Let's go," I called out once more before climbing in the car, this time in the passenger seat.

One time in the driver's seat was enough for me for one day.

He didn't say anything else before getting behind the wheel.

I fastened my seat belt extra tight. The feeling of it digging into my lower stomach was comforting. It brought me a sense of relief in an uncomfortable situation.

My breathing became a little ragged when the engine roared to life. I felt a tingling sensation in my feet and hands. I just wanted to get home as quickly as possible and in one piece. Glancing out the window, I tried to focus on anything I could to steer my mind in another direction.

"You know I still think you should be the one to take care of me. After all, you did break my nose."

I snapped my head in his direction. His eyes squinted as if he was mad, but the smirk on his lips said otherwise. He was picking another fight with me.

Turning my head back towards the window, I smiled where he wouldn't see me before I fired back at him.

"And like I said, you have a mother."

"A step-mother," he corrected.

"Same difference." I rolled my eyes at him.

"Hell no, she's a witch. I'd be better off taking care of myself. Besides, she's not the one who broke my nose."

"You are such a baby," I replied. He was being awfully honest about his stepmom. It sort of took me by surprise. We don't know each other well enough to be spilling our darkest closet secrets, and he was damn wrong if he thought I'd ever tell him anything about my life. "You know, I'm going to need you to fix my door before my parents come back home, so you better ice that nose and heal yourself quick."

"I'll fix the damn door, but you're going to take care of me first. If you want me to work, well then you'd better see to it that this swelling goes down."

God, he was a sarcastic asshole.

"I've seriously had more than I can handle for one day," I said. I watched him drive the car with ease, though he probably couldn't see well over his profusely swollen nose.

"I won't be much trouble. I won't even talk. I'll let you continue watching your scary movies on the couch, while I sit there in pain."

I couldn't be certain, but it seemed like he was avoiding going home. What was I supposed to say to that? He was a grown ass man, shouldn't he have had an apartment in the city or some place far away from here by now? That was what most people did. They graduated from Suck-Ass high school, left this Godforsaken town and never looked back. He left once. I was almost positive. So why did he come back?

The car rolled to a stop in my driveway. We made it back in one piece, and all it took was a couple of arguments. I was proud, and exhausted.

"Are you going to let me come in?" He asked. This time there was sadness in his voice.

"On one condition..." I started, and he nodded his head. "No talking, no whining, and under no circumstances do you expect me to take care of you. You're a grown man, and that broken nose was coming to you."

He sighed. "That's a whole lot more than one condition."

"Sue me." I opened the door quickly and climbed out in need of the fresh air that wafted across my face. His footsteps fell in sync with mine as we made our way up to the porch. "Can you please fix this door tomorrow?" I pointed at the barely shut front door. My parents were going to flip out.

"Yeah," he replied. "Thank you," he said stopping me right outside the door. He was inches away from me, and closer then I wanted him to be. It was uncomfortable and unnerving.

"You're welcome," I replied quickly. I started to walk through the door, but I had something else to say. It was hard for me, but we'd already spent a lot of unnecessary time together and I wanted us to be honest with each other. "Look," I said. "I'm not sure why you don't want to go home. I don't know why you would want to come here, and not stay with someone you know, but whatever. I'm not going to ask you about your situation, so don't ask about mine. I'd like to stay on a mutual –not giving a rat's ass agreement. Understood?"

"Yep," his eyebrows rose, but he didn't say anything back. He just followed me into the living room taking a seat on the small couch.

I flipped the television on, turning the sound down to a bearable number and left him sitting there as I walked into the kitchen. I needed a minute for whatever reason. I sat down at the kitchen table and rested my head on my folded arms. My brain had far too much going on inside, and I needed to decompose. I had to relax. I felt tired, and weak. Just a little peace and quiet would make me feel more in control.

I pulled out my hearing aid and laid it on the table. The relief I felt at having it out was amazing. It was like shutting myself off from the world. After a few minutes and after feeling like I was in full control again, I was ready for the couch and my movies.

Walking back into the living room, I was just about to ask Will if he needed an icepack. I said I wouldn't take care of him, but the doctor insisted that ice would help the swelling. I didn't mind making him one.

I walked around from the backside of the couch and found him slumped over onto the armrest asleep. The pain medicine must've knocked him out. He looked uncomfortable with his back hunched over. Not sure where the goodness inside of me was coming from, I pushed him back and situated him the best I could so that he'd be more comfortable. He never stirred as I lifted his legs onto the small couch. He was far too big for it, but we'd make it work. His legs weighed a ton, but I somehow managed to get them up. I used the couch blanket to cover him up, and left him sleeping soundly. He was so sweet when he slept, aside from his mouth hanging wide open. I guess he couldn't breathe through his broken nose. I laughed at his heavy breathing, but tried not to linger. I would hate for him to wake up and find me staring at him. That would've been awkward.

I climbed back into my makeshift bed on the big couch and lay down, this time with my head closest to him.

"Shit," I grumbled. I needed my hearing aid in case something went wrong while he was sleeping.

I walked back into the kitchen and grabbed it from the table. I positioned it back into my ear before heading back to the couch. If anything happened, I didn't want to be scared shitless again, or break another nose. I lay back down on the couch and stared at the television. I wasn't really watching, more like replaying the day's events.

What a day this had turned out to be. I'd need a week to recover.

I closed my eyes for a moment, but sleep soon found me.

***

I woke up to a missing Will. The couch was empty, and the blanket I'd given him was folded neatly over the back of the couch. I hadn't even heard

74

him get up, which was weird since I fell asleep with my hearing aid in.

I rubbed the sleep from my eyes, and stretched my arms wide above my head, stifling a yawn.

What time was it?

I stood up from the couch and looked at the clock behind me on the wall. It said 6:05 A.M.

Holy crap.

I'd slept all night, and most of the morning. I must've been exhausted because I never slept that much.

Ever.

It was unlike me to sleep more than three or four hours at a time.

My belly rumbled letting me know it was past time for food. I was just about to head into the kitchen for some food when I found Will's note folded on the coffee table.

England,

I found the hardware I needed to fix your door in my Dad's garage, so I'll be over later today

to fix it. Here is my cell number. I wasn't sure when your parents would be home, but I didn't want to wake you this morning. Just call me whenever it's a good time to come back and fix it.

Will

P.S. Thanks for the couch and the blanket. It was the best night of sleep I've gotten in a long time.

That put a smile on my face, which felt far too unfamiliar. It meant that I was actually having a good emotion that was related to another human being. It felt weird, and in many ways wrong.

I shook it off.

After I stored his number into my phone under Pain In My Ass, I texted him instead of calling. I wasn't ready for that yet. I told him that I'd be home all day, and that he could come back anytime after I'd had my

76

shower. And a shower was the first thing on my agenda. Well, after food.

He texted back with a simple "okay" followed by a smiley face emoji.

Of course, I had to send him the devil emoji back because I wanted him to know that I wasn't a smiley face emoji kind of girl.

He returned with an LOL.

I blew out an enormous breath before sliding my phone across the kitchen counter.

Holding my bowl of cereal close to me, I carried it up the stairs to my bedroom. That was something else I wouldn't do if my Mom were home. I probably wouldn't even eat breakfast if she were there. Any way that I could avoid the weird confrontations between us, I did.

I scarfed down the cereal like I hadn't eaten in weeks, and hurriedly undressed for the shower. I needed to get in and get out before Will showed up.

Thirty minutes under the hot stream did wonders. So not exactly in and out, but it felt good. I wasn't ready to face the world again, but I felt decent enough to go downstairs and chill out for a while. I loved not having my parents at home. It meant I didn't have to stay so secluded. Too much time in my bedroom was lonely and depressing. That was why I snuck outside most nights. Even just hearing the sounds of nature could pull me out of my funk enough to stand it.

While I was in the shower I thought about what Mom had said about getting a job. I wasn't even sure what made me think of it, but if I ever wanted to get away from this place then I knew I would have to eventually find a job. I didn't want to be there, hidden away in my room for the rest of my life. But I didn't want to be out in society either. Maybe I wanted to be hidden away in the room of my own home, but I couldn't do that without a job. The thought of it was so scary. Could I ever do it?

Maybe I just wanted to be a lazy bum on the outskirts of society forever.

Now *that* I knew I could do.

It would be fun explaining that one to my parents. She'd have a conniption fit, and I'd probably be out on the streets before I could even finish telling her. It was the hardest thing in the world not having my sister, but not having parents too... I could hardly stand it. If I was going to be on my own, then I truly wanted to be on my own.

I flipped the light switch off in the bathroom before the mirror could look at me. I didn't want to see it. I never wanted to see it. It was always her that glared back at me, and that wasn't the way I wanted to remember her. As heartbreaking as it was to say it, I really never wanted to remember her. It was unbearable. It would feel like someone was driving a stake straight through my heart. That was why I couldn't look in the mirror. It scared me to death to see it. She was gone, and I could never talk to her again. I could never hug her. I couldn't even tell her goodbye.

Ugh!

The tears sprang free from my eyes, just like they did every time I thought of her. I was drowning in them, and this place, this house was my graveyard. The more I thought about being here forever the more it broke me. I always thought that this was my safe place to fall, that I'd get by here.

I was wrong.

I had no intentions of getting better by being in this house with my sister's memory. My parents were mentally not there, and I was mentally glued there. I was on the verge of losing my damn mind.

It's funny how a thirty-minute shower after a day in the outside world could make a mind change. I slept better on that couch last night then I had in months. I wasn't alone. I wasn't in my room all night replaying the same nightmare in my mind over and over again. I'd slept more than four hours, and I didn't wake up in a screaming fit. I'd made it through a whole night, and it was the first one since my sister had died.

I walked down the stairs to find Will standing in the doorway working. I stood there lost in myself just looking at him.

It was like everything clicked all at once. It wasn't the good night's sleep, or the shower. It was Will, the goofy, smartass man that made me talk. He made me drive. He made me interact. He made me feel.

And at that moment I was feeling more than ever wanted to.

He glanced up at me with his two black eyes, and smiled. But his smile turned into a worried expression.

"Are you okay?" He asked.

"Uh, yeah. I'm fine." I lied. I wasn't fine. First I was crying, and then I thought I had a breakthrough, then he smiled at me, and I felt like I could throw up.

Shake it off.

I cleared my throat. "Will you be done soon?" I'd changed my mind about him being there. It was too much. I felt like someone had placed a plastic bag over my head and I was struggling for air. I could feel the burn in my throat as I tried to swallow.

"I shouldn't be long." His eyes narrowed. "Do I make you uncomfortable, because I thought we were past all of that when you broke my nose?"

"Ha, ha, very funny." I replied, trying to ease a bit of the tension. "I broke your nose because you're a smartass. And yes I'm uncomfortable." I answered honestly.

"Okay." He held up his hands. They were covered in dirt and dust. His eyes searched for mine, finding me staring back at him. He nodded his head letting me know that he understood. Whether or not he did I wasn't sure, but we were amongst some kind of agreement. There was a slight tilt in his head and he spoke once more. "I'll be as fast as I can."

"Thanks," was the only word I could find in my nonexistent vocabulary.

He didn't say anything else. With his back quickly turned, he proceeded to work.

Flipping on the television to break the silence, I made myself comfortable on the couch tucking my legs closely into me. It took a few minutes for me to ignore the fact that he was still in the room, but I finally did. I was engrossed in the T.V. and away from my thoughts.

8

Will

England was like a hot flash. One minute she was fine, and the next minute she was sweating bullets. I couldn't keep her cool, not matter what I did.

After the awesome night of sleep I'd gotten and the funny text she sent me this morning, I thought things were going well.

Boy, was I wrong.

I felt my phone vibrate inside my pocket. Fishing it out, I realized it was my Dad, and I knew I'd better take the call. I stepped outside to the front porch to answer the phone.

"Hello," I said.

"Where the hell are you at?" He jumbled into the phone.

"At the neighbors doing some work. I'll be home in a little bit."

He cursed under his breath. "Boy, there's work to be done here. You can't just live in this house rent free."

Here we go again. He acted like I was some kind of a burden to have around. I never interfered with their business, and I was hardly ever home except to sleep. It was times like this that made me miss my Mom a hundred times worse. She would never treat me the way that he did even if I was a child, which I wasn't.

"I know that. I'll be home as soon as I can."

He hung up the phone without saying goodbye and I just shook my head.

Daddy dearest...

Searching through my phone contacts I pressed on Jace's name.

"Hey man," he answered.

"Hey."

84

"What's up?" He asked.

"I need a place to crash for a couple of nights." I pleaded. "I hate to be a pain, but my Dad is being a real ass and I don't have anywhere else to go. It'll just be for a night or two."

"Yeah man. You know I don't care."

"Thanks, bud. I'll call you later before I leave the house."

I ended the call, and put my phone back into my pocket.

When I walked back inside the house England was still sitting in the same place that I left her. I didn't bother her, because I had enough on my mind. I went back to working on the door.

Living with my Mom for so many years, made me pretty handy. I was always the one to fix things around the house. All she had to do was ask, and I did it. So a job like this was a breeze with the right tools. The difficult part was doing it with a broken nose. I couldn't bend over without feeling like my head was full of bricks.

And sneezing…. Bad idea.

I almost took another pain pill afterward. It hurt worse than the time I got a two-inch splinter in my ass cheek. Talk about an embarrassing conversation to have with my Mom. She just laughed it off though, but I couldn't look her in the face for a week.

Glancing back at England, I thought maybe she'd feel me looking at her. That she'd turn around to see what I was up to if I stared long enough, but I got nothing. She was either ignoring me, or so engrossed in her T.V. show that she couldn't look away.

It was probably wise of her to stare at the screen, and not look back. Someone with as many issues as she had, didn't need the baggage that I carried. Besides, I wasn't in the right frame of mind to be getting so emotionally attached to someone. I was never the attached kind of guy. I was the lick em' and leave em' type.

I placed the last of the screws back into the doorknob and tried it out. It opened. It shut. And it was a nice job.

I tiptoed to the side of the couch and waited for her to look up. She had her hearing aids in because the T.V. was at a normal volume.

"Got a broom?" I asked when she looked up at me.

She rolled her eyes before she got off the couch and stomped away. It was typical England behavior and it made me smile. She always made me smile even though she was being a complete pain in the butt.

I was crouched down on the floor picking up the tools when the straw end of the broom hit me on the leg. She didn't even give me time to say thanks before she walked back over to her couch and plopped down. Sometimes she reminded me of a teenage girl who didn't get her way, and other times she seemed like a badass girl with an "I'll break your nose" attitude. There were more sides to her than the dice on a craps table.

Sweeping up the dust off the foyer floor, I hoped it wouldn't make me sneeze. That's the last thing I needed.

I sat the broom up against the wall and grabbed my toolbox. I walked back around the couch and gave England a wave to let her know I was leaving. I was blowing this Popsicle stand, and never playing knight-in-shining-armor again.

Surprisingly she waved back, but I didn't waste time analyzing it. I closed my wide-open jaw and walked out the door, hoping that she wouldn't cross my mind again. I knew it was a lost cause, and hoped that just maybe some booze would cure it.

I needed lots and lots of alcohol.

9

England

Will finished fixing the door and cleaned up his mess before he left. He gave me a simple wave without another word as he walked out closing the door behind him. That was the last interaction the two of us had in days. He didn't come back to the house anymore after that, and that suited me. My life felt fine before he came in and toyed with all of my emotions.

Okay...

So it wasn't fine.

But at least every day felt unaltered. I could go through the motions of each day expecting nothing out of the ordinary. I knew what lay ahead each day.

He'd waltzed over here unannounced and disrupted my day, and it had taken me two days to recover from it.

Thankfully I wouldn't have to worry about him anymore. He hadn't tried to call, text, or anything.

I glanced up at the clock in my room, wondering when my parents would arrive. It was their day to be back home, and it was well past suppertime. I hadn't come out of my room for the greater part of the day, because I knew they'd be home today. The awkward confrontation was too much to bear. I'd probably get a hello, and a pat on the shoulder at best.

It was dark outside and I considered turning the lights off to pretend I was asleep so that they wouldn't have to be burdened with speaking to me once they arrived. But first, I needed a cigarette.

Even though no one was home, I still climbed out of my window and down the side of the house. It was like second nature, and until that trellis gave way, it'd be the only way I left my bedroom for the outside world.

I made my way over to my favorite spot and sat down in the grass. Fishing my pack of smokes out of the wood, I lit up my last cigarette. The burning feeling as the smoke entered my lungs with the first drag was like a drug to me. It made me feel calm and relaxed; a place I needed to be before seeing my parents.

The wind made a whistling sound as if a storm were brewing. It was cool against my arms giving me chills, but I didn't mind. It felt good.

I was nearly finished smoking when a bang from behind me startled me to my feet. I looked around quickly but saw nothing. It was dark, and the noise sounded as if it came from the neighbor's house.

Will's house.

I dropped the cigarette to the ground and stomped it out with the bottom of my tennis shoe. When I glanced back at Will's house, I noticed the light was on in the room where I'd seen Will before. Another loud bang sounded and then a shattering noise.

What the hell was going on over there?

It sounded like someone was breaking all the furniture in the house.

A shadowy figure moved across the window where the light was on, and I wondered if it was Will. Was that his room?

I didn't stick around to find out.

My feet moved quickly back towards the house. With every step, my breath hitched. I'm not sure what I was afraid of. I supposed loud noises in the darkness would give anyone a fright. At least that was my excuse.

I put one foot on the trellis to climb up when I heard the sound of my phone dinging from my back pocket.

I knew it had to be Will. He was the only person that would contact me. It never made a noise otherwise. Not even my parents would call or text my phone. I don't even know why I had one in the first place. Not anymore.

I glanced back behind me to the open yard before looking at my phone.

-Don't go in yet?

I looked around once more; for fear that I was about to get the life scared right out of me. Will's message was direct, and a bit odd.

The phone sounded again, just as I was contemplating whether or not I should stay.

-Please

I stayed right where I was, next to the house, and waited for Will. Something was wrong. I could feel it down in my bones, like a sixth sense or something. He needed me to stay, and I did. It was different than when he needed me to stay in that hospital room.

I could hear his footsteps in the distance as he made his way closer towards me. I kept my phone in my hand just in case. I wanted to be certain it was his face that I was about to see, and not some masked murderer.

Clearly, I'd watched too many horror films in the past few days.

I took a few steps towards the front of the house when the footsteps grew closer.

"England, it's me." Will's deep voice confirmed it was him.

I released the breath that I wasn't even aware that I'd been holding.

"What's going on, Will?" I asked. My voice was slightly shaky.

"I saw you sitting outside, and I wanted to talk to you," he replied.

"Cut the crap. What's going on? Your message was far more direct than just needing to chat for a bit."

He ran both hands down his rough, non-shaven face, wincing as his fingers touched his bandaged nose.

"I had to get out of the house," he admitted.

I crossed my arms over my chest to keep the chill away. "I heard," I said. My voice was uneven. "What's going on?"

"Look," his tone was clipped. "I don't want to talk about it. It's fine. I just wanted to get out of the house, and I didn't want to be alone."

I could live with that, although I did want to know what was happening. I didn't ask again. He hadn't asked me about why I was such a fucked up mess. I had no right to ask him.

"Okay," I answered. "Do you have any cigarettes?"

His frown faded. "No. They'll kill you."

I tossed my head back and let out a loud sigh, pinching my eyes closed tightly.

"My Dad has a couple of beers in a cooler on the back of his work truck."

"Finally," I reacted. "Now you're speaking my language."

It had been a very long time since I'd had any alcohol. My parents didn't keep any in the house, and since I never left, there was no way of ever getting ahold of any.

"Do you want to walk with me?"

I was a bit reserved seeing as all the noise had been coming from his place.

"Uh, I guess."

"Are your parents back home yet?" He asked.

95

I fell into step beside him. "Not yet. They're supposed to be home sometime today. I haven't seen them yet."

"Will they be worried if they come home and you're not in your room?"

"No," I said sternly.

He didn't say anything back. I was kind of liking this whole –let's not talk about our pasts or anything much related to the present thing we had going on.

Using one of the old wooden posts of the fence, he hoisted himself over it with a jump leaving me on my side. I was uneasy about trying the same maneuver. There was no way I'd clear that fence with my short and stubby legs. I wouldn't be as graceful either if I tried.

"I'll wait right here."

"Come on," he smiled. "I'll help you."

He reached his hands out over the fence as if he were going to pick me up and hoist me over it.

"Yeah, that's not going to happen."

"Oh come on. You're not afraid are you?" He challenged me with his eyes. "There is an ice cold beer waiting for you on the other side."

My shoulders sagged in defeat.

Every single time he was present I found myself in situations that I otherwise wouldn't be. He was like a fuse to a firecracker. He sparked interest, burned quickly, and set off an explosion inside me.

"I'm too heavy."

"Jesus England! You couldn't weigh more than a hundred pounds soaking wet. Come on." He waved his hands for me to move closer. "I got you. I promise."

There was something about the way he said the words –I promise- that made me believe him. Or maybe he was just the most persuasive person on the planet. I couldn't be sure.

I inhaled deeply and stepped the last couple of feet into his arms. He tucked them under my armpits like he was about to lift a child, and I silently thanked God that they weren't sweaty. That would've been horribly embarrassing.

"When I say three, you jump."

I nodded, placing my hands firmly on his hard shoulders. "Don't drop me Will."

"I won't. One, two, three."

Up and over I went. He picked me up like I was light as a feather, and sat me down easily on the other side. He didn't let his hands linger on me. He gave me the space I needed.

It was okay.

It wasn't so bad.

One hurdle at a time...

"Thanks," I said.

"You're welcome. This way," he replied.

We walked along side of each other until we reached an old pickup truck, which I assumed was his Dad's. He climbed on the back and opened a cooler grabbing us some beers from inside. "Victory," he proclaimed.

Just as he was climbing down, another loud noise rang from inside his house. This time, it sounded like a wall coming down. It was loud and thunderous, and it made me jump at the sound of it.

I could faintly hear yelling from people inside. I didn't know who it was, but I could make out both a male and female voice.

"Come on," Will jumped down off the truck and hurried back in the direction of my house.

I couldn't be positive about what I was hearing, but if I had to guess then I'd say they were fighting, and it was probably his parents. Or his father and his stepmother I should say. It was scary to think about it. At least my parents got along with each other.

I often thought my home life was miserable, but maybe it wasn't so bad after all. They didn't speak to me much, but it would be better than listening to that all the time.

Stop it England.

I was always jumping to conclusions. I didn't really know what went on in Will's house, but if that was any indication then I felt sorry for him.

"Hold these beers in your hand, and I'll lift you back over the fence." He handed me the three beers he swiped from the cooler. He stood behind me and placed his hands on either side of my waist. After counting to three, I was back over the fence on my side. I still had a firm grip on the beers.

He jumped back over and took the beer from my arms before popping a squat on the ground. His back was against the wood and he'd opened a beer before I even sat down.

"Here." He handed me one as I made myself comfortable. "I'm sorry about that," he said.

"It's none of my business," I responded. I didn't look at him to gauge his reaction, but I knew that he was upset or maybe even embarrassed. He had every right to be, but I wasn't judging. It wasn't my place.

"No matter. I wasn't thinking when I asked you to walk over there with me. I didn't want you to hear that. Hell, I don't want to hear it. I've had enough of that shit." He proceeded. "They've always been like that, and it doesn't even phase them."

I didn't respond. I figured whatever he was saying was just something he needed to get off of his chest. The words poured out as if they'd been itching to get out of him and be free.

"I didn't want to come back to this house. I never wanted to hear them fighting again." He took a long drink of his beer, and rested his head back against the wooden post.

I glanced at him for a long minute and watched as he kept his eyes firmly shut. He was mad or sad. I didn't know. What I did know was that he was alone, otherwise he wouldn't be sharing this stuff with me.

"I'm not trying to pry Will, but why did you come back here. I mean to live with your Dad."

He replied with calmness in his voice. "My Mom died."

I looked down at my lap. I didn't want to cry, but I felt like I might. Instead, put the glass bottle to my lips and drank every last drop inside it.

He was hurting, and I knew pain like that. I was hurting too. I didn't tell him that I was sorry for his loss, because I didn't want him to say it to me. Instead, I scooted over to him where my right leg touched his left one, and I laid my head over on his shoulder. It was all I could give him for the pain. It was all that I had in me to give.

We sat like that for a long while without speaking. I never looked him in the face, but I think he understood what I was giving him. In a world full of pain, we had each other in that moment. No matter how brief it was I silently thanked him for never pushing, for opening up to me, and for getting me a beer.

Maybe Will wasn't so bad after all.

10

Will

I told her my Mom died. I just blurted it out, like I'd been holding my breath for days. The feeling of releasing those words was like letting the air out of an overinflated balloon. My chest felt a little looser, and my head didn't hurt quite as bad. It wasn't the alcohol talking either, because I hadn't consumed enough beer to even give me a buzz. It was just me letting go of my troubles.

Since my Mom had passed, I hadn't really talked to anyone about how tore up I felt inside, or how broken it had left me. There was no one to talk to that would take me seriously or even give a damn for that matter. So while sitting there with England, in the moment, it just felt right. For the first time, I felt like I could say the words that I'd wanted to say for months.

My mom died.

It was odd to me that she'd be the one person I'd tell it to. Ironic actually.

Luckily, she didn't ask any questions. She just took my hand in hers and laid her head on my shoulder. It was the most perfect thing for her to do.

Slowly, I moved my head lower to rest on top of hers. I could smell the shampoo scent in her hair. It smelled like vanilla, soft and sweet. Closing my eyes and taking a deep breath, I knew that I would never forget the way she smelled in that exact moment. Her hair blew loosely around her face and touched my cheek, and it took all the power I had inside me not to lift her lips up to mine. I wanted to. I never wanted to kiss somebody so much in whole life. There wasn't a doubt in my mind though, that me stealing a kiss would end with another punch to my nose.

My nose, and my pride couldn't take that.

Her head was still resting on my shoulder when I spoke. "This has got to be the most quiet moment I've had in a long time."

"Was," she replied lazily.

"Huh?"

"It was the most quiet moment. You ruined it when you opened your pie hole."

I laughed, and her head jarred against my shoulder. "Right."

I wish I could've seen her face. I wanted to know if she was smiling too. Her sense of humor was one of her greatest features. She didn't even know she was funny, but she was. She was quick witted, and sarcastic. It suited her.

My eyes grew heavy, and I let them close as we sat there in silence. I wondered what she was thinking, and if she felt as comfortable in the moment as I did.

Just as I was about to doze off, a car honked loudly causing England and I both to jump out of our skin. Behind me, I could see Jace's pickup truck in my driveway.

"Shit," I said. "He's going to piss off my Dad. I have to go."

We climbed to our feet, and England brushed off the back of her pants before picking her beer up off the ground. "I have to go too."

That was all she said before she turned and stomped off towards her house. No goodbye, or see ya later. She didn't even tell me to go to Hell.

"Hey, England!" I called out for her, fully expecting her to keep walking. But she didn't. She turned around and looked at me.

For a second I stood there in shock, looking at her like an alien had invaded her body. Then Jace honked again.

"Dammit Jace!" I yelled. "I'm coming."

"What do you want Will?" England placed her hand on her hip, and I wanted to scoop her up and throw her smart-ass over my shoulder.

"Nothing," I grumbled.

I swear I heard her grumble too before she spun around to walk away.

106

Shaking my head at her, I turned around and jumped over the fence to head back to my place. I'd forgotten all about telling Jace to come pick me up, and I wish I hadn't. I could still be rested up against the fence with England.

"Will," Jace yelled out the window. "I brought you a present."

Glancing back towards my front door, I checked to make sure my Dad wasn't standing at the door. The way Jace was honking and yelling, Dad should've been out there with his baseball bat. He must've been passed out already.

I opened the door to Jace's Chevy and climbed inside. He had the truck lifted up so high that you'd have to jump if you were average height. Lucky for me I was six-foot.

"Hey Will," a girl's voice caught my attention. When I turned around, both Robin and her best friend Skyler were in the backseat.

I wasn't expecting them.

Jace raised his brow at me. "I told you I had a present."

"Ladies," I said before turning around in my seat. Their high-pitched giggles made me want to scratch my corneas with sand paper. Clearly they were several bottles ahead of me with their drinking, and I wished I had some excuse to stay home as Jace backed the truck out of my driveway. The only problem with staying home was that my Dad was there. I couldn't win, so I clenched my jaw and stared out the window.

"Where we going, man?" I asked over the loud roar of the engine.

"We're meeting Daniel and Melody at Winchesters."

I glared at him. That high-faluting club was not my idea of a good time. I hated that place. Melody's Dad was some big time member there, and when we had nowhere else to go, that's where we'd always end up. Only because we could eat for free.

Jace turned the radio up and started playing the drums on the steering wheel. It was our thing. If Daniel were here he'd be whistling the tune, while I played air guitar. The three of us were the best band you'd ever heard that didn't have instruments. Jace tapped my shoulder and when I looked at him he was playing the drums hard, and I knew it was my cue to come in with the bass solo.

I couldn't be a sour puss all night.

I scrunched up my face, curled my lip, and then I got down to business. I played a better solo then *John Paul Jones of Led Zeppelin.*

At least that's what I told myself.

Too bad I couldn't play a real instrument if I tried.

When we pulled up to Winchester's, I quickly climbed out of the truck. I was already in a better mood than before.

We walked around the side of the large brick building and through the black iron gate to the patio. Melody had a special table that was always reserved near the pool area in case we wanted to swim, or more so when someone decided to throw someone else in. We were like a wild pack of animals, and I swear we got away with everything when we were there. I just assumed her father practically owned the

109

place, but I never asked. Sometimes it could be fun there, but it usually ended up with someone vomiting in the bushes, the very expensive bushes.

"Hey," I tipped my head at Daniel who was already tipping back the champagne bottle. He'd already drunk enough that he no longer needed a glass.

I was way behind.

"Will, hey," he called out my name. "How's it been, man?"

"Same as always. Pass the bottle." I held out my hand. "You missed one hell of a bass solo on the ride over."

He laughed. "That's too bad. One day when we're rich and famous and about to open for the Stones, I'll look back on this moment and feel proud that we were once the greatest air band of all time."

I spit my champagne all over the place. Daniel was always the jokester. "You want my autograph now?"

Daniel pretended to bow to me before tipping back the bottle. He was my closest friend, and lately he'd been so preoccupied with Melody that we never had any time to just hang out anymore. We hadn't watched a Panthers' game together all season. It was kind of depressing. He was the one person that I kept in touch with when I moved in with my Mom, the one who helped me pack up her house after the accident. The two of us had known each other since elementary school.

"So tell me what you've been up to since you're not working anymore?" He asked me.

"Not a lot." I looked down at the ground below me. I hadn't told him anything about England. Not that there was anything to tell.

"Something's up," he sneered at me.

"Naw. Just tired of my Dad's bullshit, but you know that."

He nodded, but didn't ask anything more.

"Melody!" He yelled out, calling his girl over. She was a pretty thing, and clearly head over heels for Daniel. I was happy for him. She was one of the only girls in this group that didn't annoy the shit out of me.

I figured that at any given time they'd be settling down and getting married. That's how serious it was.

Daniel pulled her down onto his lap and kissed her cheek.

Suddenly, I was missing England.

I pulled out my phone and typed a text to send to her. It took about five long minutes of staring at it before I erased the whole damn thing. I was drunk, but I had a feeling that I'd regret my words tomorrow. Besides, we were barely just friends. I didn't want her thinking that I really was a stalker. She was one of those girls that if I wanted, I'd have to take my sweet time with. She was as fragile on the inside as they came despite her badass attitude.

Thinking about her put this ridiculously stupid grin on my face, and I realized then that I needed a second bottle of the disgusting champagne.

11

England

At five a.m. I checked my bedroom door only to find that the clothes had not moved. I had no idea if my parents were home, but if they were they hadn't been upstairs to check on me.

It was the same as usual, just a new day.

I didn't give it another thought. I threw the covers off and climbed out of bed. Stretching my arms wide, I could feel the stiffness in my body release. I put in my hearing aid and left the room to go downstairs. Before I even made it to the kitchen, I could hear the rustling of papers. I assumed it was the newspaper. My Dad liked to read it in the mornings. Which meant that my parents were home, which also

113

meant that I was correct in assuming that no one had checked on me.

Go figure.

"Dad," I said which was code for –good morning.

"England," he replied, which was code for - same to you. He glanced slightly in my direction before turning his face back to his paper, never looking at me.

I grabbed a slightly brown banana from the fruit basket on the kitchen counter and started to leave the room.

"We need to talk to you," my Dad said. I thought maybe I was hearing things. His sentence had more than three words in it, so surely he wasn't speaking to me. I turned around quickly. His eyes caught mine in a brief moment of clarity, but like I said it was brief.

I remained standing in the spot where my feet were firmly planted. I couldn't make heads or tails of any of it. There was no logical reason why my parents would want to speak to me, unless they were finally kicking me out.

I felt my heartbeat pick up with all the worry that washed over me.

That was it. They were finally kicking me out.

I had no job, no money, and no place to go.

"England," my mother said as she walked into the kitchen. "Come sit down."

I flinched at the sound of her high-pitched voice. My hearing aid hated her tone. It was as bad as nails on a chalkboard.

The wooden chair scratched across the floor as I scooted it out to sit down. I let my eyes roam my mother's face for some clarity about the situation, and I found it. Her face was easy to read. She was dreading the words that were about to leave her mouth. Her lips were drawn tight together, and her dark brown eyes creased in the corners.

"I asked for a relocation at work. We're moving to Atlanta in three months." She stared down into her coffee cup. I tried to get some kind of a response from her, any kind of response, but there was nothing.

"What does this mean?" I asked, but I already knew the answer.

"It means that your father and I are moving."

And there it was. Nowhere in her words had she included me.

"So let me get this straight," my voice sounded aggravated, because I was. I had every right to be angry with my parents. They'd shown me zero attention since the accident. They didn't care if I was even alive. Obviously, they wished that I would've died instead of my sister and they weren't the only ones. I'd been wishing that since the day it happened.

"You're both moving, and I'm going where? To hell," I groaned.

"England," my Father growled. I was taken by surprise because it was the most emotion that my Dad had shown me in a long damn time.

"We can't stay here any longer. It's too hard for us. If we are ever going to move on with our lives, then we have to move." Again my mother's voice annoyed me to death. And she had still not looked up from her coffee cup.

116

"I have no job, no money, I don't have anything, and I'm assuming you weren't planning on taking me with you?"

She gripped her mug tightly. "No, we weren't. Your Dad and I feel like you're an adult and you should be moving on with your life too. It's time you got back out into the world and started doing something with your life. I suggested that you get a job, because you can't sit in this house anymore."

I bent down trying to get her to look up at me, but she wouldn't. "You can't stand to look at me, either of you. And you're giving me this lecture about moving on. I don't buy this crap. The only reason that you're leaving this town, and this house is because you can't bear to look at me. Do you know how that makes me feel? I'm so fed up with the two of you acting like I don't exist. I am still alive you know! It's bad enough that I can't even look at myself in the mirror, but you two won't even glance in my direction. I'm sick to death of it. Why don't I just say what everyone in this room wished for? That I was dead instead of Elise."

My mother flinched at my harsh words, but I didn't care. I was only speaking the truth.

"I might as well be dead, because the two of you already act like I am." I was fuming mad. My hands were shaking and I wanted so badly to rip that coffee mug from my Mom's hands and smash it into the ground.

"England, you're acting like a child," my Dad said, without one single bit of remorse.

I slammed my fists into the wooden table, and jumped up from my chair. "Thanks, Dad," I said with a fierceness that I'd never felt before. "I'm sure as hell glad I'm not a child, because if were, you might actually feel ashamed at the way you've treated me. I'll be out of your hair soon enough, and you won't ever have to worry about seeing my face again. I'd hate for things to be too hard for you." I said sarcastically as I stormed out of the kitchen.

Instead of going back upstairs to my bedroom, I walked right out the front door and slammed it behind me. I took a left as I stepped off the porch, and headed directly to the fence. Only this time I didn't stop. When I spotted Will's car, I marched off in the direction of his place. I don't know why, but I suddenly felt the need to see him.

Instead of knocking on Will's door, I tapped on the window that I saw him in before. It was so early in the morning and he was probably asleep. I tapped lightly one more time before backing away from the window. I didn't want anyone else in the house waking up because of me.

I was just a few feet away when I saw someone peek through the window blinds.

The blinds closed back up, and within a few seconds, the window was opening. Will, with his half-opened eyes poked his head outside.

"Hey, what are you doing here?" He asked.

There was a sudden realization that I must have looked like an idiot standing outside of his window so early in the morning. I stuttered over my words before the right ones came out. "I didn't have anywhere else to go, and I couldn't stay home," I admitted.

"Come on," he threw his head back for me to come over there.

For a second I almost chickened out, but one thought of my parents and I knew I couldn't go back home yet.

He raised the window up far enough where I could climb inside, and I did. I maneuvered myself through it, and into his bedroom.

Once inside, I realized that he was only wearing a pair of tight fitting boxers.

Oh, they were tight.

I had to look away for fear that my face would give away the embarrassment that I was suddenly feeling.

He realized why I wasn't looking and responded with, "I'm sorry. I was in bed." He walked around to the other side of his queen-sized bed and grabbed a pair of loose shorts from the floor. He didn't seem bothered at all that I was seeing him in nothing more than his underwear. Or maybe he was still half asleep.

I took a good look around his room as he was pulling up his shorts. It was nothing like mine. The furniture was mismatched, and there were lots of pictures on his dresser. The room was painted light blue, not like sky blue, more like barely-there-blue.

"You want to talk about what's going on?"

I shook my head no. All I wanted to do was forget that the whole thing happened in the first place, but I knew that would be unlikely.

"I'm sorry I stormed over here unannounced. I just…" I sighed. "I didn't know where else to go. I don't really have any friends to talk to."

"Stop. It's okay." He walked back around the bed to where I was standing. "I'm your friend."

I gazed into his sleep filled eyes. He was so nice to me, and I didn't know why. I didn't deserve his niceness, far from it actually.

Glancing down at his bare chest, I couldn't help but stare. He was a hot guy, and it wasn't the first time I'd noticed.

"You want to sit down?" He asked, forcing me to break my eyes away from him.

The only place in the room to sit down was his bed, but I didn't hesitate. "Thanks," I replied.

I sat down on his bed and felt the mattress dip beneath me. His covers were strewn all over the place, like he rolled around in them or as if he hadn't made his bed in a week.

"I don't sleep very well," he smirked when he noticed me staring at his bed sheets.

"Me either," I admitted. "The last time I got a full night's rest was when you slept over."

"Seriously? Me too. I slept better on that tiny ass couch then I've slept in months."

I smiled. It's funny how the both of us had slept so well when we were complete strangers. It felt right, though, and not at all hard to explain. Maybe we barely knew each other, but I felt closer to him than I did with my own parents.

"It's really boring here, especially at this time of morning. Nights are usually so much louder," he explained, and I knew what he meant. "The morning is so quiet, it's the best time for me to sleep."

Of course it was. "I'm sorry Will. I can go and let you get some sleep. I wasn't thinking." "No. Stay. Please. I don't want you to go. You must be tired too. We could sleep here together."

"What?" I quickly glanced at him like he'd grown two heads.

"Sleep, just sleep," he said waving his arms around like he was pleading for me to understand. "Not that I wouldn't sleep with you the other way, I just... Damn it, I'm still half asleep now."

I smiled shyly at his cuteness. It was the first time since we'd started talking that I felt we'd had such a sweet moment. It felt real, and nice. It didn't scare me like it had before. This time, I was thankful to be given such a good friend in my time of need. And as an added bonus, he was very good looking.

"Will you get in trouble for me being here?" I asked.

"No, and I'll lock the door so you don't have to worry about anyone coming in. Deal?"

"Okay," I agreed.

Will walked over to his bedroom door and turned the lock. When he walked back over to the bed, he slowly climbed under the covers. The entire time he never took his eyes off me. Maybe he was worried that I was worried, but I wasn't.

I wasn't worried at all.

I lay back onto the pillow and pulled the blankets over me.

"Thank you," I whispered.

"You're welcome."

His hand touched mine under the covers, and instead of pulling away, he grasped it with his. Our fingers interlocked and stayed that way as the two of us drifted off to sleep.

***

"England," I felt myself being shaken awake.

When I opened my eyes, Will's face was only inches away. It startled me for a second. I was a breath away from feeling the stubble on his cheeks brush against mine.

124

I blinked quickly trying to wake myself up. It felt like I hadn't been asleep very long. I wasn't ready to get up just yet.

"What is it?" I asked. My voice was hoarse as I spoke.

"It's after lunch and I'm starving. I feel like my insides are about to start eating their way out."

"Nice visual." I rubbed my eyes. Did he say lunch? "I can't believe we slept so long. I can't believe I slept at all." I couldn't hide the smile that crept up on my face. There was something about sleeping in the same room as Will that made everything better.

"Come on," he smiled.

A part of me would have rather curled back up under the blanket, but he was persistent and adorable with his messy bed head.

He held out a hand to me, and I took it. "I'm up," I said as he pulled me into a sitting position. Wiping the sleep from my eyes, something caught my attention. Out of the corner of my eye, I saw my sister. It sounds crazy, but it was her.

When I snapped my head harder to the left, I realized I was mistaken.

It wasn't her.

It was me.

My reflection was staring back at me from the mirror attached to Will's dresser.

Fuck!

It felt like the wind had been knocked from my lungs with a baseball bat. I squeezed my eyes tightly shut and threw myself back onto the bed.

I couldn't look at her.

I couldn't look at me.

I couldn't breathe.

I curled myself up into the fetal position and willed the image to go away.

"England," Will said in the distance. It sounded like his voice was calling me from the far end of a tunnel.

"It wasn't her. It wasn't her. It wasn't her," I repeated. My eyes filled with unshed tears, and the air slowly refilled my lungs so that the breaths didn't burn as I sucked them in. "She's dead," I said to myself.

"England, please," Will's voice became clearer, like he was closer. A warm hand touched my cheek, and I slowed my breathing. But I wasn't ready to open my eyes yet.

These things didn't happen in my house, because I made sure that I avoided every mirror we had. Avoidance was the key.

My eyes fluttered as I opened them slowly.

There was a look of pure torture on Will's face as he looked at me closely. He dropped his chin to his chest, and I could see it moving quickly with each breath he took.

"I'm sorry," I said. My voice was shaky.

His large hand cupped my cheek and he looked at me with nothing but concern.

"I'm sorry," I repeated the words because I felt so bad for making him witness my crazy episode. It was bad enough that I had to feel the pain. I didn't want him to have to feel it too.

He wrapped his arms around me and pulled me firmly to his chest. His hands held me tightly and cradled me to him.

A hug.

He hugged me.

I never knew how much I needed it, but I did. The tears fell. I couldn't stop them. His embrace was like the key that unlocked my heart. It had been locked up so tightly that nothing was allowed inside or out. With the tenderness of his touch, it unlocked. Every horrible, hurtful, agonizing feeling that was held tight inside of me emptied.

I felt raw.

It scared the shit of me.

But mostly I felt alive, and that was the scariest feeling of them all.

I buried my face deeper into Will's chest, and let him hold me.

"It's okay. Let it out." He rubbed his hand down my head and said soothing words to me as I continued to cry like a big ol' baby.

Once the tears went away and my eyes were nearly swollen shut I felt him pull back. "This is deep. I didn't realize, and I'm sorry."

"Don't," I stopped him, placing my hand gently over his. "Please." My eyes pleaded with his. I was thankful the crying fit was over, and I certainly didn't want to relive it through his eyes.

He nodded his head before standing up. When he started walking in the direction of the mirror, I kept my head down. I didn't want to risk seeing it again.

"You can look now. I covered it up."

Glancing in his general direction, I saw that he'd covered up the mirror with clothes. Probably dirty ones from the floor, but I didn't care. It was gone. Suddenly the room didn't feel quite as suffocating.

The silence in the room surrounded us, but it was okay. We didn't have to speak. I was just glad that the uncontrollable sobs had finally stopped.

Out of nowhere, Will's stomach growled and broke the silence. Not just an ordinary growl, it was loud enough that it sounded like a bear clawing its way out of him.

His blue eyes grew wide and a smirk played on his lips.

"You'd better eat before that thing inside you finds its way out," I pointed to his stomach.

"Come on, let's go out to eat."

My hand grew tight around the blanket.

Out.

To eat...

I didn't like the sound of that.

My breakdowns should be minimized to once a day. Once was my limit.

"Can't we just eat here?" I reverted back into the fetal position. It was the safest place for a girl on edge.

He plopped down, belly first, onto the bed next to me. His cheek was resting on the palm of his hand, and those eyes of his were narrowed at me. I hated that look.

Technically it was the first time he'd given it to me, but I didn't like. It was the same look my sister used to give me when she needed me to cover for her, or when she was trying to convince me to do something I wasn't in the mood for.

I recognized those closely squinted eyes, and that pouty lip.

"You know drives aren't my thing, and neither are people. I prefer the hermit life," I pleaded.

"So we'll go through a drive-thru, that way you don't have to talk to anybody. I'll even let you flip people off at the stop signs. Come on, please." That lip of his was stuck out where it clearly didn't belong.

I sighed. I could feel myself breaking under his gaze.

"You don't have to drive," he said. "And I'll argue with you the entire time.

"Fine, you win. Let's go."

"Thank you. I'm craving a double cheeseburger and tater tots." He waggled his eyebrows before hopping off the bed. He was too eager for me, but I liked where his head was. I could taste that cheeseburger already.

As I was fixing my ponytail, I watched Will ditch his dirty tee shirt back onto the floor. The muscles in his back moved as he bent down and pulled a clean shirt from his dresser drawer. There was something about his back that I found attractive.

Crazy I know, but those back muscles led to his stomach muscles and he was built like a Trojan horse.

Bad reference.

It was more like an athlete or a knight who had no need for any armor.

I'd tried desperately not to think of him in any way that would form some kind of attachment, but I couldn't help myself. I knew a great set of back muscles when I saw them. He was too hot not to notice, and I was a female with intense hormones that even painkillers wouldn't cure.

Snap out of it!

From post collapse to raging slut, this day was one for the books.

Just last week I was unable to move beyond my fence, and today I was ready to hop into Will's car, and take the road less traveled. Who would've guessed?

Not me, that's for sure.

"Let's go. I plan on driving too fast and listening to the wrong radio station too loud." He draped his arm over my shoulders and led me out of his room.

I rolled my eyes. "I'm fully prepared to fight about it the entire way there."

"Can't wait," he replied teasingly.

"Don't be cheeky." I laid my head over on his chest.

"You love it when I'm cheeky."

I pinched his side and felt him jump next to me. I wouldn't dare tell him that I do love it when he's cheeky.

12

Will

I could seriously get used to having England in my bed. It felt like I never knew what sleep was until she showed up. Seems crazy, right? That just having her near me would make me sleep better. There was no way to describe it other than pure effing bliss.

The massive hard-on she gave me was the only downfall. It ached, but in a good way. She made me feel like a man, and I knew I wanted her more than anything. My tight shorts proved it.

Behind the wheel of my Mustang, I buckled my seatbelt. England fidgeted with her hands from the passenger seat, and I immediately felt guilty for putting her back in the car. Maybe I was pushing her boundaries too quickly. I wanted her to ultimately feel like she could trust me, but I could never take no for an answer. I shouldn't have pushed her into doing something that she didn't want to do.

At that point, it was too late. I had her there and I'd see to it that she was okay. I'd take care of her.

There was something my Mom told me about girls when I was about twelve years old. I couldn't remember her exact words, but I know she said that one day I'd meet a girl that would infuriate me beyond belief, but that she'd be the only thing I could think about. I thought my Mom was crazy, but she wasn't.

England was that girl for me.

13

England

Once we were back on firm, familiar ground, I felt like I could breathe easier. He'd taken me through the Sonic drive-thru and allowed me to complain to the boy who took our order. Oddly, the two of us were a screwed up match made in Heaven.

We popped a squat next to the fence line nearest his house. I stretched my legs out in front of me, and waited for him to pass the bag of tater tots that he'd been holding hostage.

My fingers gripped the bag, but he wasn't letting it go that easily. His stern grip left me glaring daggers at him. In return, he had a devilish grin on his face.

"What?"

"You're getting better." He said, his face inching closer to mine.

I felt my breath catch in my throat, as he grew closer to me. Time stood still the instant his eyes caught mine. "At what? Fighting?" I replied breathlessly.

"Yes, and trusting me," he whispered softly. His eyes stared deeply into mine, and then drifted aimlessly down to my lips. Just maybe he was about to kiss me.

And I was going to let him.

My lips parted, and my heart raced. This was the moment, or so I thought.

Just as his lips grew close to mine, he popped a tater tot between them.

Poof.

So much for the perfect moment, the little slime ball was playing games.

I narrowed my eyes, and clenched my jaw.

He laughed. He laughed so hard that I thought he might choke on his food.

"Glad you think that was funny." I could feel my face glowing red.

"Aww, don't be so glum. If I'd known you wanted to kiss me that bad, I'd have taken advantage days ago." He winked.

What? I could feel the anger inside me. "You're an asshole." I moved quickly to try and get away. I didn't even want to look at his face for another second. If he thought he could mess with my emotions than he was dead wrong.

"Wait," he grabbed my arm pulling me back to the ground. "I love it when you're angry."

His lips crashed into mine with force. At first, I tried to pull back, but the heat of it sucked me in. He coerced me into anger the same way that he had done when we were in the car. Well... maybe not the same way, but he was just trying to get a rise out of me, and it worked.

The battle inside me was over, and I kissed him back just like I wanted to. I kissed him hard, and with everything I had. I wanted him to feel it all the way to his toes.

The heat of the moment had hooked me, and I never wanted our lips to part. I wrapped my arms around his neck pulling him closer to me. I let my lips move in sync with his as I took everything from him that I didn't even know I needed. I was opening myself up, and I never wanted it to end. His hand snaked around my back squeezing me against him, while his lips devoured me.

I hadn't played this moment out in my head, but even if I had, it wouldn't have compared. There was a spark; a feeling that I never knew existed. It was real, and I needed real.

A soft moan escaped my lips, and he eased his grip. His lips kissed me gently once more before they parted and our foreheads rested gently together.

"Wow," he said through his deep breaths.

"You're forgiven," I smiled.

He returned the smile before closing his eyes. It felt good knowing that he felt it too. That this wasn't just some kiss between two random people. It was much more.

I wasn't looking for this in my life. I didn't even know I wanted it, but it felt right.

And if there was one thing I learned from my sister, it was that you couldn't help how you felt. She said it all the time.

Your feelings don't lie.

I remember exactly how she said it too, and that she meant it with all her heart. She was a believer in love, and fairytales. I wasn't. But Will didn't happen upon me by chance. I could feel it all the way to my bones. He was real. And my feelings for him were real too.

Our bellies were full, and Will's Dad and Step Mom had finally left the house. Meaning, we were free to go back in. Thank goodness, because I didn't want to listen to the two of them fight, and I knew how uncomfortable it made Will. He didn't say it did, but it had to.

He offered me a hand to stand up from the ground, and I took it. We hadn't said any more about the kiss that happened between the two of us, but there was nothing to say. It was easy to see that he liked it as much as me, and with our fuddled up lives, there was no need in adding more to think about. In my opinion, it was like keeping it sacred.

I walked through the front door this time instead of climbing through his bedroom window like I had before. It opened into a living room with dark red walls and gold border. There was a leather sofa, and recliner, as well as a flat screen T.V. that looked like it used to hang on the wall.

Used to, those were the key words, because the wall had a massive hole in it instead.

Will caught me staring at it with wide eyes.

"No one was harmed in that incident." His eyebrows were raised and his lips pinched tightly together.

"Good," was all I could say in response, as I let him lead the way back to his bedroom?

Stopping briefly outside his kitchen he said, "There is a mirror in the hallway."

I nodded.

"Just look down at your feet."

I did what he asked, and scoffed when I noticed the giant hole in the big toe area of my sock. I'd been all day and night in the same pair since I ran out of the house without my shoes. Will didn't seem to mind, but I was a bit embarrassed by the sight of them. I shimmied them off in a hurry as I followed closely behind him down the hallway.

Well shit...

I don't know which was worse, no socks, or unpainted toenails.

I shook my head. Since when did I care?

"Since the frog became the prince," I said under my breath.

"What was that?"

"Uh, nothing," I said, keeping my head down as we stepped inside his room.

"You know what?" Will turned to face me.

"No, what?" I hesitated.

"I want to take you some place."

"I'm not really in the mood to fight again, and that's what will happen if I get back into that car of yours."

He grinned. "Where I want to take you doesn't require the car. How do you feel about four wheelers?"

I tilted my head to the side giving him a questionable look. "I don't know really. I think I was about ten years old the last time I was on one."

His eyes glowed with excitement. "Come on. No time like the present."

"Wait," I grabbed his hand. "Could you give me some socks without holes in them?"

"I don't wear socks," he replied seriously.

"Who doesn't wear socks? That's gross you know. I bet your feet smell like ass," I joked.

He crouched down like he was about to pounce on me. "Why don't you smell them and find out," he growled just before tackling me to the bed. I was in a fit of giggles as he playfully rolled me around.

Out of breath, Will leaned down and kissed my lips taking the last little bit of air I had. And I let him. I gasped just as he released me staring up into his blue speckled eyes.

"Socks are in the bottom drawer, but be careful. I'd hate for your beautiful feet to smell like ass."

"Very funny."

He kissed my nose and waited for me to put on a pair of his extra-large gray tube socks, and then he led me to the garage.

***

I thought I'd be scared. I thought I would feel completely under pressure with that four-wheeled machine between my thighs, but I wasn't. It didn't scare me like I thought it would. It was actually fun. I didn't have to worry about other people crashing into us, and Will didn't drive it fast enough for me to freak out. I could see myself doing it again.

Talk about surprising.

I kept my arms tight around his waist as he pulled up and stopped by a small creek on the back of his property. The water trickled over the mossy rocks and you could hear it running once the engine was cut off. It was peaceful and secluded. The tall trees that surrounded us offered shade from the hot sun.

My eyes grew heavy as we sat there in silence. I wondered how I never knew that this was even back here. It was obvious that it ran along the edge of my property too, but I'd never seen it before today. Maybe I never had time, or took the time, to find it. Before the accident, my life was busy. I only made time for myself and what was important to me, and at that time the only thing of importance was what my plans were on the weekends. Though my sister and I had different personalities, we were both teenagers with the simplest worries. They used to seem big, but after losing her it seems I didn't even know what worry meant.

"What are you thinking about back there? You're awfully quiet." Will's hand gently brushed my knee.

"My sister actually. I miss her a lot." I admitted.

145

He caressed my knee gently leaving goose bumps where his fingers touched my skin. "I don't know exactly how you feel, but I know I miss my Mom too."

I was sure that he did. Good or bad, no matter the relationship, losing a parent couldn't be easy.

"What happened with your parents?" He asked, not giving a shit that he was prying into my personal life. "You don't have to tell me, but I wish you would."

Stupid icing on the stupid cake...

His "nice" voice was too damn nice.

"What do you want to know?"

"Why you came running to me," he answered too quickly. It was like he'd been holding that question in just waiting for the right time to ask me.

"Deflate your ego, because it's not like you're hot or anything," I joked. His body shook with laughter. Of course, he knew I was playing around. "My parents are assholes. Since Elise died neither one of them will look at me." I admitted to the seat of the four-wheeler that I was looking at. I pretended that I was alone when I said those embarrassing words.

146

"The same way you won't look at yourself."

"Don't go there. This is different."

"Right," he replied sarcastically.

"I'm serious. I can't look at myself in the mirror because I see my sister. Those are my parents. I'm their kid. It's not just the fact that they don't look at me; they also don't talk to me. I may as well be a ghost in my own house. Now they want to move out of the freaking state and they don't want to take me with them. They said it's time for me to move on with my life, just like they were. Only they're not moving on, they're running away."

They were cowards.

"I have nowhere to go. I'm alone in a world where I can barely function. I can't look in the mirror. I hate people. I don't like going places. All I want to do is hide, and they're not going to let me. Of course, they're not going to let me. Why make things easier for me, you know?"

"You're not alone," Will said. He rose up onto his feet and kicked his long leg over the seat until both feet were on the ground. Reaching for my hand, he helped me off the four-wheeler and led me to the edge of the slow-moving water. The cool breeze made me move in closer to his side, and without wavering, he wrapped an arm around me. "I'm sorry your parents are assholes. You don't deserve that. It's sick really, and I didn't mean to be a dick about it."

"You're entitled to your opinions." I sniffed trying to keep my nose from running.

"Maybe so, but I have no right to judge anyone. Who the hell am I?"

I wanted to say that he was sweet, and kind, and even though he annoyed me that I'd be lost without him. I was too chicken to say it, though. You may as well have glued the feathers on my rear end, because when it came to emotional feelings, I had no idea how to express them. I'd learned from the best seeing as my family didn't exactly sit around campfires singing Kum Ba Yah.

I sighed heavily and watched the water trickle over the rocks. I wanted to relax and let my worries run away like the water, but it wasn't happening. In a matter of days, I'd be homeless. What was left of my dysfunctional family would be miles away and long gone. It was like waking up from a bad dream to find that the dream was real and that there was actually no waking up from it.

"It's one big nightmare," I groaned. "I know I need to go home and talk to them so that we can work this out, but it's so hard facing them. I couldn't get one single reaction from them earlier. You should have seen that far off look on my Dad's face. It was like talking to a wall. No, not even that. A freaking wall would have had more emotion than my Dad. I'm just over it. And you know what's even more pathetic?" I asked.

I didn't wait for his response.

"Every night when I go to bed, I place a pile of clothes against my door so that in the morning I could tell if either of my parents had come to check on me. Every damn morning the clothes are still against the door. They've never moved. I'm such a naïve idiot."

"Stop okay," he leaned his head over to rest on the top of mine. "You're not a loser."

"I said idiot, not loser," I laughed.

"I know." I could feel his smile even though I couldn't see it. "If you need a place to stay, you can stay with me."

I hesitated. The fact that he was asking was a shocker.

The tone of his voice was not very convincing and if I had to guess, I'd say it was out of pity. He didn't owe me anything, and I wouldn't have felt right about accepting unless maybe I was accepting as a friend.

No. No. No.

"I don't think so." I shook my head, and released myself from his arms so that I could see his face.

That wasn't a good idea.

It was a very bad idea.

Sweet Lord, he was easy on the eyes, and even more so when he was serious.

And he was serious.

I could see the muscle tighten in his jaws.

"I mean it. I'm not leaving you out in the streets. You have a place to stay if you need it. Besides, I sleep better when you're in my bed."

I bit my lower lip to hide the smile. "Now I get it. You only want me cause you sleep better." I giggled. "Ahhhh," I yelped as Will grabbed my hand and pulled me to him.

"I do sleep better when you're there."

I had goose bumps all over, everywhere but my teeth and it wasn't because of the cool air.

He bent down slowly and painfully, and placed a light kiss on my lips.

Once.

Twice.

Three times.

"Say you'll stay with me." He kissed me again.

I couldn't open my eyes because I knew that the world would be spinning if I did.

He paused; his lips so close to mine that I could stick my tongue out and touch them.

"Say it," he whispered.

"I'll think about it."

151

Opening my eyes, I found him with a wide cheesy grin.

In the blink of an eye, he smacked my ass and hoisted me over his shoulder. "Time to go, sweet cheeks. You've got a meeting with your parents and I want you back in my bed tonight."

14

Will

Freaking hell.

Her kisses were like a drug to me. I never wanted to stop doing it.

Not ever.

She walked across the driveway towards her house, and I hated seeing her go. I knew that this meeting with her parents would be awful. The way she described them to me made my stomach turn. You don't just cast away your child because you've lost one. You don't just forget that they ever existed. It's sickening.

I really wanted her to take me up on my offer of staying with me. There was no doubt in my mind that I could take care of her. I'd protect her, and I'd never treat her the way that they did. She'd feel safe here with me.

When we were out on the four-wheeler earlier and she was talking about her sister, I wanted to tell her more about my Mom. So badly I wanted to tell her. But I couldn't. She could never know about that night.

Shaking off the unnerving feeling, I went to the kitchen for some food.

"Dad."

It surprised me to see him sitting at the kitchen table. His eyes were glassed over and he sat with his arms folded at the table.

He didn't answer me.

"Where's Terri?" I asked. She was also known as Step-Mom.

"Out," he growled.

I didn't bother asking anymore because he was clearly in a fowl mood. I walked past him to the fridge and grabbed the stuff to make myself a sandwich. Laying it out on the bar, I looked over and Dad's eyes were glued to the table. Something was up with him,

154

something different than normal. Usually after a fight with Terri, he'd be on the couch with a beer watching sports.

After I finished putting my sandwich together, I sat down in the chair across from him. He didn't look up. I was getting worried. This was typically the time when he'd curse at me for eating up all the food in the house and not contributing.

"You okay Dad?"

His eyes narrowed and the pain was clearly visible.

"Terri's pregnant."

I dropped my sandwich onto my plate and glared at him. He had to be joking. She was over forty years old. She was a heavy drinker like my Dad, who enjoyed scratching her nails down the side of his face.

"You're shitting me right?"

"Nope," he shook his head. "She just found out."

"Didn't the two of you just have a knockdown, drag-out fight?"

I was seriously confused. The two of them couldn't have been that stupid.

"That's none of your business," he snarled.

I could feel the aggravation building up inside me. "She was drunk just a few days ago. She was so drunk that I found her passed out in the bathroom the next morning. She can't have a baby. Neither of you can have a baby. This is sick."

He slammed his fists down on the table and stood up. I had no idea what he was about to tell me, but I knew I didn't want to hear it. So I scooted the plate away from me and stood up from the table.

"I've lost my appetite."

The door to my bedroom made a loud slamming noise when I released it behind me. I'd never felt more furious in all my life. How could they be so stupid? There was no way in Hell that the two of them were fit to be having kids. There had to be some kind of law that wouldn't allow it.

I ran my hands through my hair, and let out a loud growl.

I felt sorry for the child that wasn't even born yet. The man wasn't a father to me. He never had been. It was going to be worse this time around because he couldn't go a day with getting so drunk he couldn't function.

Pulling the pillow from the head of my bed, I placed it over my head and screamed inside of it. I wanted to punch something, but boy would there be irony in that.

My thoughts went to England, and I wished she were there in the bed with me. I wanted my mind to be anywhere else at that moment.

STUPID. STUPID. STUPID.

Why did my Mom have to die? She was the good one. She deserved to live.

Not him. He was a piece of crap. He was a horrible Dad, a horrible husband, and a horrible human being.

I couldn't stomach being stuck in that house with him for a minute longer. So I opened the window in my bedroom and climbed out. I strode over to the fence and climbed over. I just wanted to be in her spot, even though she wasn't there.

My legs were stretched out in front of me and my back rested against the fence post. The light to

England's bedroom was out, so I figured she was somewhere in that house facing her parents. Somewhere she was probably feeling about three inches tall because they were disrespecting her.

I use to think that I'd love to be anywhere but in that house with my Dad, but I wouldn't want to be in her house either.

Too bad I couldn't just scoop her up and run away with her.

We'd leave this place, and these people, and just start fresh somewhere no one knew our names.

15

England

I had to wait until almost eight o'clock before my Mom and Dad were both in the house at the same time. Dad came home early, but stayed in the garage. I don't think he even knew that I was home. Probably didn't care either.

Mom strolled in after dark around seven thirty, but she went straight to the shower. I waited patiently for them to notice that I was sitting on the couch, but they didn't. They were best at avoidance. She walked straight through the front door, past the couch I was sitting on, and hauled ass to her bedroom. No eye contact, no hey-hello, nothing.

159

They had to eat sooner or later, or I assumed.

I waited for both of them to step foot on that linoleum floor and I pounced, like a T-Rex on a chunky kid.

"No more ignoring me. We need to talk," I said in the sternest voice I could muster up. It wasn't quite as good as I would have liked for it to be, but it worked. You could've heard a pin drop in that kitchen.

I cleared my throat. "I'm upset. Clearly," I rambled. "You're supposed to be my parents. You're supposed to care about me. Y'all act like I don't exist, and now you're leaving town and I'll probably never hear from you again."

"You're being dramatic," my Mom chimed in. "You're an adult."

"Now I'm an adult." I rolled my eyes. "Now..." I laughed, literally. It's funny how earlier I was acting like a child. "This is bullshit! Just pack your bags and go. I don't need this anymore. When I needed you, you weren't there. And now that I'm practically begging you to stay, you could care less. Is that what I have to do? Beg?"

"England," my Dad said. "The decision has been made. It will do you some good to get out on your own. Get some freedom, some independence."

It was pointless to try. I could have gotten down on my knees and cried alligator tears and it wouldn't have mattered.

"I've got some place to stay. Thank goodness. Have a great trip. Don't forget to send a postcard. Oh wait," I said sarcastically. "You won't know where to send it to. Peace out."

I seriously threw my parents the deuces. Don't even know where I learned it, but it was perfect. Just the send off that I needed.

I marched out of that house and didn't look back, and I made sure to slam the door too, rattling the windows behind me. I took a deep breath and decided not to shed a tear.

I had one place to be and it wasn't there.

"I'm coming, Will."

16

Will

"I take it the talk didn't go well." I took her hand, and helped hoist her into the window.

"That's the understatement of the year. It completely blows my mind that my own parents have thrown me out like a piece of trash. Our relationship wasn't perfect, but before the accident at least our dysfunction worked." I gripped his hand with force as my thoughts drifted. I could remember a time in the past that I could share simple day-to-day memories with them. I remember when my Dad took me for a driving lesson, and how we argued the entire time. But in the end, I learned to drive. And how my Mom used to make chocolate chip cookies and her, my sister and I would eat them in the living room while we watched old re-runs of Full House. Granted, it was a weird relationship, but it worked. At least I felt like I had someone. I didn't feel so alone. I know that I'm acting like a pissed off child. I get it. But I feel like I have a right to. They could've at least said –hey, we're moving and you can come stay with us until you get on your feet. They could've told me that they'd give me a few months to settle and get a job until I found a place. But NO! Instead, they tell me they're leaving the state and I'm not going with them. I swear I could break something."

"Not my nose again," I said placing my hand over my face.

She balled up her fist and waved it in the air. "I'd look out if I were you," she joked.

"Come here," I pulled her to me. "Let's go to bed and get some sleep. In the morning we can figure out our next step. I don't want to be stuck in this house forever. Maybe the two of us could find some place to rent."

"You're kidding right?" She narrowed her eyes at me. "You can't be serious?"

"I'm not kidding," I replied seriously. "I have money saved up from when my Mom passed away. I also have her house, but I don't think I'm ready to go and live there. I was just staying here with my Dad so that I wouldn't have to be alone for a while. It's hard not having my Mom, even if it meant listening to all the damn fighting around here. But I'm ready to get out of here, and you need a place to stay. It could work for us."

I was as serious as a heart attack. I wanted her with me. If I were going to dive into the whole living together situation then I couldn't think of anyone I'd rather do it with.

She shook her head, but she never said anything. I couldn't tell what she was thinking. Naturally, she probably thought I was crazy, and maybe I was, but I wasn't alone on this crazy train.

I rubbed her arms. "We'll talk about all of it tomorrow. Right now I just want to spoon you in the bed."

"Spoon?" She smiled.

"Yep, now get in."

She climbed into my welcoming arms and I wrapped her up tightly keeping her as close to me as I could. I could smell her shampoo again, and I inhaled deeply. It was so familiar, and soothing. I couldn't get enough of her.

Her body was warm up against the front of me, and I gently rubbed my hand against hers. I let my lips gently brush her neck and she sighed, making it hard for me not to flip her over and kiss those lips of hers.

As we lie there quietly, I felt her breathing slow as she quickly drifted off to sleep. It took only minutes for her. She was exhausted.

I kept her wrapped up in my arms for the rest of the night and felt more at home with her than I'd ever felt in that house with my Dad.

17

England

I was growing used to the good night's sleep that I'd been getting in Will's bed. But this time, it was different. Will had forgotten to lock his bedroom door, and his very angry father woke us up.

I had my hearing aid out and could still hear him so he must've been screaming. I startled awake, and pulled the covers tightly up around my neck letting it cover me completely. I wasn't naked underneath, but his intimidating stare was scary. I could see it through the glow of the light in the hallway.

The light in his room was switched on, and I quickly reached for my hearing aid off the bedside table, scrambling to get it into my ear as quickly as possible. There was a bit of panic in me when I saw the look on his father's face. There was rage in his bloodshot eyes.

Will stood up from the bed putting himself in the sightline of his father's eyes so that he wasn't staring at me. Will was a bit taller than his father, but not enough to make him relent. His father continued to scream at him as he moved himself closer into Will's personal space.

I was frightened; scared that he'd do something crazy like hit Will or maybe me.

"You ungrateful son of a bitch, bringing your whore into this house!" His dad screamed.

I gasped, but not at his words. Will had his father by the neck and pushed him up against the wall. It was all happening so fast, and I couldn't find a voice inside my throat anywhere. Not that I'd know what the hell to say. I was freaking out.

"Don't you ever call her a whore again? Do you hear me?" Will was snarling at him.

There was no response.

"You're a sick son of a bitch, and you're lucky I don't break your face right now."

Still, no response…

I rose up on my knees and peeked over Will's shoulder, and that's when I realized that his father wasn't able to speak. Will was choking him to death. Literally.

"WILL, STOP!" I yelled, but he didn't move. "Will, please." I scrambled to his side. "Don't do this. You're hurting him. Let him go," I pleaded.

His eyes finally met mine, and I could see the pain and anger in them.

"Just let him go. It's not worth it."

Will let go of him, and I heard him suck in a hard breath. Another minute or two, and he would've been unconscious.

His father scrambled backwards and through his staggered breaths he said, "Get out." His voice was scratchy. "Get out, of my house."

Will snickered. "No problem. I'll be gone in an hour."

He slammed his bedroom door in his father's face and then kicked it.

I flinched.

"I'm sorry."

I knew that he was. I knew he was just defending me, but I didn't want him to get kicked out of his house. Not for me.

I was nobody.

That was his Dad.

I touched his arm gently. "Will," I tried to speak to him.

"No." He shook his head. "Don't look at me like that. This was not your fault. He was going to kick me out sooner or later, so don't go blaming yourself for this. I was leaving anyway."

Swallowing the lump in my throat, I nodded. There would be no arguing with him in the state he was in. He needed me to be on his side, to agree with him no matter what. So that's what I did.

"I have some more luggage in my closet, if you want to grab it. We'll get this room packed up and then we'll find us some place to go for the night."

Trying to hide the sad look on my face, I agreed.

"England," he said and I turned to face him. "Wherever we go will just be temporary until we find a place of our own."

"You sure you want me to go with you?" I questioned, needing to make sure that it was what he really wanted.

His lips crashed into mine with urgency and devoured me all the way to my soul. It was all the reassurance I needed.

We filled all of his luggage, a couple of totes, and three shoeboxes with his things. His room was practically empty besides the furniture, which he said belonged to his Dad.

Instead of carrying everything out the front door, he had me climb out the window and handed me the bags. He didn't want to face his Dad again and I didn't blame him. The man was pure evil.

Funny how the two of us had such different parents and each of them sucked in their own way.

After the car was loaded down, we climbed inside.

"Crap! I don't have any clothes or anything," I explained, and truthfully I wasn't ready to go back inside that house again. Not yet.

"If you're good for the night, then I'll bring you back tomorrow to get some things. It's up to you."

I smiled. "That's perfect. I really didn't want to go back in there. Not while my parents are still there. It would be like walking into a room full of vampires with an open wound."

His laughter filled the car. "You and your visuals."

"I only speak the truth, my friend," I said sarcastically.

The engine roared to life, and for the first time in a while, I didn't feel scared. There wasn't that deep need to breathe into a paper bag or stick my head between my knees. I just wanted to leave these two houses behind us in a trail of dust.

Will reached for my hand and held it tightly in his as we pulled out of the driveway and onto the

171

main road. His thumb gently brushed the top of my hand and I knew that he was trying to comfort me. It wasn't me that needed the comforting this time. I took my free hand and rested it on top of his so that both of my hands were closed around his and I looked at him. I really looked at him. I wanted him to know that I was there, and I could be to him what he was to me.

18

Will

"Is this alright?" I asked when we pulled into the parking lot of the hotel. I hated taking her someplace like this, but we didn't have many choices around the area.

"Will. We've been all over town. I would've been fine with the first choice. This is the most expensive hotel in town."

I glanced at her from under the brim of my ball cap. She had a look in her eyes that I couldn't quite read, but it looked like aggravation. And so, this hotel was the one.

"Fine. Let's go."

I grabbed my bag from the back seat and led us to the front lobby.

She waited a few feet behind me with her head down while I checked us in and got the keys. There were hardly any guests around at that hour, but she just kept staring at the ground. Even on the walk to our room, she never looked up. I wasn't sure if it was a fear that someone would recognize her or if she was just scared of random people catching a glimpse of her. Either way, I didn't mention it.

"This is us," I said, putting the plastic key card in the door.

"This is nice." Her voice was barely above a whisper. She looked carefully around the room taking notice of every detail. Her fingers skimmed the surface of the wooden table that was placed under the large flat screen television. I noticed her other hand was fiddling with her ear.

"Something wrong?" My hands snaked around her stomach.

"Oh," she startled. "Um."

"What? What is it?"

"It's just," she paused and sighed. "My batteries are low on my hearing aids. There is this stupid ringing going on, and it's driving me crazy. My replacement batteries are on my nightstand at home."

I kissed her neck. "Take them out."

She purred like a kitten under the touch of my lips, and I couldn't get enough. I braved slipping my tongue over the base of her neck and she nearly melted in my arms.

"Take them out," I repeated.

In a breathy voice, she replied, "I won't be able to hear you."

"I don't need you to hear me Babe. Just see me." I turned her body around so that she was facing me.

In her eyes, I could see the lust that matched mine. She wanted me just as bad as I wanted her.

"Take… Them… Out…" I paused between each word to kiss her lips.

She reached up and slowly slid the hearing aids from her ears. I took them from her hand and placed them on the wooden stand beside us.

Running my hand gently down the side of her face, I let my fingers memorize her. There was something extremely sexy about not speaking. Her eyes asked the questions that her mouth couldn't, and with every touch I knew she wanted more.

My lips claimed hers and my body reacted to her every movement. I swiftly picked her up off the ground allowing her legs to wrap around me. She locked them so tight that I could feel the warmth where our bodies touched. Her fingers ran through the hair at the back of my head and firmly she pushed our lips tighter. She was an unbelievable kisser and urgent, as if she couldn't get enough of me.

Breaking off the kiss, I looked her deeply into her eyes. I nodded toward one of the beds, silently asking her if it was okay to take her there.

She shook her head yes, and I claimed her mouth once more before laying her softly on her back a top of the comforter. Good grief she looked so beautiful underneath me. Her hair was all strewn about, her face was red, and her lips were swollen from my kisses. There wasn't a more beautiful girl in the entire world.

Her hands reached up behind my neck and she pulled me down closer to her. I found myself staring deeply into her eyes once again. I could get lost in them. Her fingers grazed over the length of my neck, and I knew what she wanted. I let my tongue graze her bare skin, and kissed every inch I could. There was a moan coming from deep within her chest, and I couldn't take it anymore. I wanted to be as close to her as I could possibly get.

I grabbed hold of the bottom of my shirt and lifted it over my head. She bit her lower lip as she watched my every move. My dick twitched under her hot glare. I rested my hands on the bottom of her shirt waiting for the okay, when she raised her arms above her head. She was even more beautiful than I thought. I couldn't keep my lips off her, and so I kissed her tender skin. I kissed the parts of her breasts that were peeking out above her bra. Stopping at the top of her jeans, I looked up to meet her eyes. My fingers paused on the button as I waited for the go ahead. She lifted her hips up off the bed giving me the silent signal to go ahead. It was the first time in my life that my fingers wouldn't work the way I wanted them to. I was frantic-mc-butterfingers. Her light laughter was music to my ears. With her head cocked slightly to the side, she gently used her working fingers to undo the button of her jeans and gently slide down the zipper.

I felt my breath catch in my throat before I slid her jeans down her hips and over her feet. I tossed them over my shoulder to the floor. My eyes were fixated on her body, taking her in completely. The sight of her undressed on the bed was almost more than I could take. It was different, different from any feeling that I'd ever had for anyone. It was real.

Instead of waiting for me, she hooked her fingers in the lacy sides of her red underwear, slowly and mercilessly teasing me before sliding them off.

I wasted no time following suit. It only took seconds for me to get my jeans off.

Crouched in a kneeling position between her legs, I lifted one of them to my shoulder kissing her gently from her ankle to her thigh, feeling her shiver

178

beneath me. I kissed her inner thigh and lowered her leg back to the bed.

Her breathing hitched when she knew exactly what I was about to do. I slowly slid a finger inside her before leaning forward to allow my lips hit the perfect spot. Using my tongue to have my way with her, she lifted her hips higher off the bed. Clearly, I was doing everything right, but I couldn't let her finish. I wanted to be inside her when she screamed out my name.

I rubbed her leg as I leaned over the bed and grabbed the condom from my wallet. She stared at me intently as I slowly rolled it on. I quickly placed myself above her gazing down at her beautiful face. Her arms reached around my back pulling me closer to her. I'd never been more ready in my life.

When I kissed her neck, she let out a soft sigh. I gently slid myself inside her and she cried out. Or I think she did. It could've been me. My hips bucked as I slid in and out of her. Watching the way her mouth moved, and the feeling of being inside her was all I needed. I pushed in and out only a few more times before I completely lost control. Our bodies shook, and I buried my head in her neck holding her as close as I could. It would never, ever be better than this, right here. She intoxicated me in the best way possible.

I brushed the hair back out of her face, as we lay there tangled up together. Her eyes grew heavy, and I kissed her forehead just before she drifted off to sleep.

19

England

I woke up very early from one of the greatest sleeps of my life. There was nothing like stirring awake to find yourself naked in the bed with Will Edmunds. He was a creature like no other, and in the buff, it was one of the most magnificent sights your eyes ever beheld.

As quietly as I could, I slid out from under his heavy arm that was draped over me. All of the heat radiating off his body had me feeling like I was inside a sauna. Additionally, I needed to pee so bad that I thought my bladder would explode.

Once off the bed, I tiptoed into the bathroom making sure to lock the door behind me. I wasn't ready for him to see me on the toilet just yet. I needed at least three more dates.

Not thinking about what I was doing, I washed my hands in the sink; the sink that had a giant mirror hanging above it. For the slightest second, I caught a glimpse of myself. And when that didn't scare me, I looked up again. Only briefly, but it was enough for me to notice something different in my reflection.

For the first time since Elise died, I could see myself in the mirror. It was a breathtaking feeling.

I sniffled as the warm tears fell from my eyes. I had to be imagining things. What could've changed?

Scared to look again, I kept my head down. I didn't want to risk being wrong. I'd have a complete meltdown if I were wrong. Of course, me crying like an idiot already probably counted as a meltdown.

Deep breathes.

My eyes remained closed as I lifted my head back up.

Closed.

Closed.

Closed.

Open.

Oh my God.

It was my reflection. I wasn't the replica of my sister anymore. She was gone.

I sobbed. I sobbed so hard that I couldn't catch my breath. I had completely forgotten that Will was in the other room, until a loud knock sounded on the bathroom door.

"England! England, open the door."

Without thinking, I quickly turned the lock on the door and it swung right open.

"What's wrong? What's going on?" He questioned. "Oh shit, the mirror!" He pulled me to him, but I couldn't stop crying. It was like the biggest weight had been lifted off me, and at the same time, it was like my sister was gone forever. I didn't really know which emotion had taken over my body. I only knew that I was upset and needed to cry.

He picked me up and carried me back to the bed, enfolding me in his body. I lay there crying my eyes out, and he comforted me through every moment.

So many different thoughts were running through my head that I couldn't keep them straight. And what surprised me the most was when I wanted to share this news with my mother. I wanted to run to her and tell her that the mirror that used to hold me prisoner didn't anymore. Of all the people I could tell, I seriously wanted it to be her.

For a solid fifteen minutes, I cried heavily, until I was all dried out.

Slipping out of his arms, I walked over to the T.V. stand and grabbed my hearing aids. The world finally became un-silent again, and Will patted the spot next to him on the bed. He wanted to talk about what happened.

Understandably.

"I'm sorry Will," I said pulling the covers up over my still naked body.

"Hey, don't be sorry. I forgot all about the bathroom having a mirror."

I shook my head no. "It wasn't what you're thinking." I started to tear up again. "I didn't see her

184

this time. I always see Elise's face staring back at me when I look in the mirror. It's her eyes every time."

"But it wasn't this time?"

"No. It was me," I proclaimed. "It was my rosy cheeks, and my small eyes. It wasn't her. I didn't know how to react. The tears just came out." I waved my arms around.

"This is a good thing, right? I'm confused." He gave me a weird look and his tousled hair fell down into his eyes.

He took my breath away.

"Well damn…" I covered my face with my hands. "I didn't get it before." I was rambling. I stood back up and started to pace the floor in all my birthday suit glory. It just hit me like a slap to face. "It's you."

His expression went too wide-eyed as he stared at me like I'd grown an extra head. "I feel sort of like a lost idiot right now because I really don't know what you're talking about, and I don't know how you expect me to concentrate when you're flashing your beautiful ass in front of me."

I felt my face flush red. It wasn't my intention to get him all worked up, but I'd had a revelation of sorts.

"It's because of you that my reflection changed. It had to be you. You make my mood lighten when you're around, and you make me do things that I'd never do. I can't feel my toes when you kiss me and I feel like I'm floating on a cloud when we are snuggled up together in the bed. It's because of you. It has to be. You've changed me."

I watched him climb out of the bed in all his glory and stalk towards me, like a predator. There was darkness in his eyes, and it consumed me.

"Are you saying that you love me babe?" His lips moved seductively.

It wasn't exactly what I was saying. I mean the words didn't actually come out of my mouth that way. But I kind of was. I did love him.

I loved him.

Shit.

I loved him, loved him.

"Do you love me?" He asked.

I nodded. "Yes," I answered breathlessly. "I do love you."

He grinned wide showing his beautiful teeth. "I love you, too."

I nearly attacked him, throwing myself at his mercy. It was an unbelievable feeling to tell someone you loved them. All the sonnets in the world couldn't prepare you for that moment.

The two of us fell back onto the bed where he kissed me over and over.

"You know something babe?" Will spoke between kisses.

"No, what?"

"I didn't change you. You just got better."

Funny how he knew exactly what to say and that he was right as rain, because I felt like the wounds were healing. I wasn't one hundred percent yet, but I was better. I was so much better.

Even more so after he made love to me again.

20

Will

Man have I got some things to tell you.

I texted Daniel on my way to the vending
machines. It was the first time I'd said I love you to
anybody. Well, besides my Mom. I felt like I had to tell
somebody. Daniel was like my brother. If I could tell
anybody, it was him. He probably wasn't awake yet
though. It was barely six a.m.

England said she was starving and wanted
breakfast, but we didn't have many options. Which
was why I was standing barefoot at the hotel vending
machines. I picked up a couple of honey buns, two

snickers bars, and two sodas. It was the best I could do.

My hands were full when I got back to the room so I kicked the locked door with my foot.

"Who is it?" England called out from the other side.

"Open the door Woman!" I replied.

"What's the magic word?"

"BIG, JUICY, LONG, HARD, MELT IN YOUR MOUTH..."

"Shut up and get in here," she yanked me inside. Her face was beet red, and she had that –I'll punch you in the nose- face.

It made me laugh. "I couldn't help myself. Here," I said handing her the breakfast.

"Ooooo, yum." She snatched the snickers quickly from the bed. "Snickers are my favorite."

I made a mental note.

"After we get done eating breakfast, I'll take you home so you can get your things. Then maybe we can spend today and tomorrow hunting for us a place for us."

"Sounds like a great plan, and I know just what I want to fight about in the car."

I shook my head.

Geez, I loved her.

21

England

Things were great. Will and I didn't make it out of the hotel room to go to my house like we said we would. Instead we spent another night together in bed without leaving the room. We even ordered room service, but I couldn't wear Will's boxers anymore. They fell to the floor every time I stood up. It was time for some fresh undies and a razor.

After moving at a snail's pace, we finally made our way out of the room.

When we got to my house, I noticed that both of my parents' cars were in the driveway.

"It's probably going to take me a while to pack up my things. Can you come back and pick me up in a couple of hours? Do you have someplace you can go?"

"Yeah, sure." Will leaned over to kiss me before I climbed out of the car, and I waved at him as he backed out of the driveway.

Opening the front door to the house, I found my Dad standing there by the window. He was staring outside, and didn't bother looking in my direction. As I was about to go up the stairs he asked, "Was that Will Edmunds that just dropped you off?"

I huffed. "Yep."

I quickly took the stairs two at a time, not bothering to listen to any more words that might come out of his mouth. Like how all of a sudden he wanted to have a say in who I was hanging out with. Not gonna happen.

The door to my room was wide open just like I'd left it. Everything was still in the exact same spot too. I don't know why I thought they wouldn't be. Just because things were changing in my life didn't mean that they'd change at home.

192

Reaching up onto the top of my closet, I pulled out my luggage set and my old backpacks that I'd used for school. I scrambled around the room gathering the most important things first. It was clear that I didn't have enough bags to take everything. Some things would have to be left behind.

Just as I was kneeling down by my bed, I heard someone crying. It was distant, but as I leaned in closer to the bathroom door it grew louder. So I gently opened the door and tiptoed closer to the sound. It was coming from Elise's room. There was a small crack in the door that led to her room and I peeked inside. My Mom was sitting on Elise's bed holding her teddy bear. Her eyes were closed. She rocked back and forth and cried as she held the bear close to her chest.

"Mom," I whispered.

She startled, looking up at me. Her eyes were red and puffy as she ran her fingers under them. I knew she'd been crying. I could hear her. There was no reason to try and hide it from me.

Wow, Elise's room looked exactly the same. The walls still had the same pictures on it, and her bed was still unmade from the night of the accident when she came to get me. Seriously nothing had changed.

I stepped closer to Mom gauging her every move. She hadn't spoken yet, and she only looked up at me one time. My hands brushed the edges of my t-shirt in a nervous habit. My mother made me nervous. You never knew what she might say or how she might react. Catching her in tears must've thrown her off her game because she seemed to be just as nervous as I was.

"Are you okay?"

Her eyes skimmed my face, and her expression changed. She nodded before gazing back at her hands.

I kneeled down on the floor next to the bed where she was sitting. It was the closest I'd been to her since the accident, and for good reason. After a few minutes of silence, I decided to try and talk to her. Like really talk to her, the way that we used to. It couldn't hurt trying. I was hours from being out of her life for good anyway.

"You can tell me what's going on, you know. Even if you don't want to look directly at me," I proclaimed.

I saw her tense up next to me. "You're leaving."

What? Of course, I was leaving. "You told me to leave. You said I needed to find some place to go because you and Dad were moving. I had no choice in the matter. Remember?"

"I know, but..."

"But what?" I tried to sound sincere. I wasn't trying to pick a fight with her.

She took a deep breath. "Once we're gone, you'll be gone too. I won't have anybody."

I wanted to throw something across the room, or punch something really hard. I didn't though. I kept my composure. She was toying with my damn head. "Again," I said through gritted teeth, "you and Dad were the ones who told me to go. I wanted to pack up my things and move with you wherever you were going." My voice started to rise above the tone I was trying so hard to stay at.

195

"Not me. I didn't want this. I wanted you to go. It was your Dad. He said that you'd never get better if we didn't give you some tough love," she said.

"Now I think you're completely full of shit." I cursed at my Mom. Climbing quickly to my feet, I started to pace the room. I was so close to losing my cool that I needed to keep moving. "Tough love," I repeated.

"The doctor said that we should go about things normally, as if the accident didn't happen. He said for us to move forward with our lives."

"It's been months since the wreck. Neither one of you would look at me or talk to me. You made me feel like I was worthless and didn't deserve your love. You never spoke to me at all. We didn't just go about life like things were normal. That was not normal. This is not normal. You can't tell me that it was all Dads' fault. You wouldn't even come check on me at night, no matter how many times I put that pile of clothes in front of my door. You never invited me to watch T.V. or ask if I wanted to help with dinner. You know, the way we used to do. Every single time I

196

passed one of you in the kitchen or the hallway, you wouldn't even glance up. Don't get me wrong; I knew it was hard for you to look at me. It was hard for me to look at me. I had to turn the light out in the bathroom so I wouldn't see her face when I walked by the mirror. Ugh," I growled.

She cried harder into her hands, making me feel like I was only two inches tall.

"Explain it to me, Mom, because I'm not understanding here."

She used the sleeve of her shirt to wipe her face before she said anything. "After Elise died I thought life couldn't go on. I cried myself to sleep every night praying that I wouldn't wake up, because it hurt so severely. I couldn't look at you. You're right. It tore my heart into pieces every time I had to look at your face, because you looked just like her. Your Dad kept telling me that things would get better, and they did a little. The other morning at the table when we fought, it was the first time I actually saw you and not her. I think it was because you raised your voice, and it was something I knew Elise would never do. When work offered me the chance to relocate, I thought it would be the best thing for all of us. Maybe we'd get the fresh start we deserved and I wouldn't have to deal with people staring at me in the supermarket or the pharmacy. I thought it would be good. I thought that with time, I could finally begin to look at you and talk to you. Which is something I know I should've been doing from the start, but I just couldn't. Your Dad suggested that we move without you. He said that you were old enough to make it on your own, and that the doctor was right when he said a little tough love wouldn't hurt. We fought about it for days. I told him that I couldn't lose you too, and he said it would only be temporary. He said you'd get your life straightened out, and we would all go back to normal, but I knew it wouldn't be true. I saw how hurt you were. I knew that the moment we moved away, I'd never see you again. That's not what I wanted.

I know I'm a horrible mother, and that I shouldn't have been so ugly to you, but I want to make things better. Us moving won't help."

I dropped down to my knees and tried horribly to catch my breath. This couldn't be happening. It was all wrong.

For the first time in my life, I considered throat punching my own parents. Not that I would. I'm not that horrible, but I felt the need to punish them. And hug them.

Geez Louise.

"All this time," I huffed. "I get it. I do, but I'm freaking mad right now. I feel like I've just been sucker punched in the gut and then knee-capped all at the same time." I explained. "I just wish we could've talked about all of this a long time ago. You're about to leave."

"I don't expect you to understand, but I do expect you to be mad. I needed time, and space. I needed to grieve. I just didn't go about it the right way. Not that there's a right way. And I really think your Dad meant well."

A laugh escaped me. "He meant well?" I said it more like a question. "There's no point in trying to rectify the wrongs now. I just want things to get better."

"Then go with us," she suggested.

"I... I can't. I'm getting better every day, and I can't go. I don't want to go now. Besides, Dad wouldn't want me there."

She shook her head. "Of course he would. I'll talk to him. We'll figure it out. I'll even yell at him if I have to. I just... I've already lost one daughter. I can't lose you too."

Deep down inside I wanted to tell her that she already had. That their stupid, selfish ways had pushed me right out the door. But I couldn't. I longed for this moment for months. I wanted so desperately for them to want me around, for them to love me the same as they used. Why couldn't I just tell her that it was too little, too late?

I reached for her hand, and she didn't pull away. She was my mom, no matter what. She made horrific mistakes, but that still didn't change the fact that I'd always need her.

"I want to be a family again more than anything, but I can't go with you. I want to continue to fix myself. I want to work hard at getting my life back on track. I'm ready. Or, I think I am. I don't know, but I'll never know unless I try. This is my hometown. This is where Elise is buried, and I want to be as near to her as I can. I know I'll leave this place one day, but not yet." Mom's hand still rested in mine. "I'll come visit you, and maybe we can actually do some mother-daughter things before you leave. I want that. I really do."

"Where will you live?" She asked.

Instead of admitting the entire truth, I fibbed a little. "With a friend."

"You have a friend?" She smiled though her face was tear-stained. Suddenly it was like old Mom never left.

"You want to help me pack?" I asked.

"Sure."

She followed me through the bathroom and into my bedroom.

"England," she said.

"Yeah, Mom." I continued picking random things off my dresser.

"I did check on you at night, after I sat for a while in Elise's room."

I looked back at her over my shoulder.

"You just didn't notice because I came in through the bathroom."

22

Will

I'd been all over town to pick up some things
we needed, including food. I just didn't want there to
be any reason for us to leave the hotel room. My plan
was to stay in there for at least the next week.

When I pulled back into her driveway, I got out
and walked up to the front door. Her parents' vehicles
were still there, and I was a little nervous about
knocking on the door. I mean, they knew she was
leaving. They practically kicked her out.

As I was standing there about to knock, the
door swung open in haste. A tall man with gray-
streaked hair and glasses, stood there looking at me
like he might just shoot me.

Didn't England say her Dad owned a gun?

I was just about to say hello when the man started screaming at me.

"YOUR MOTHER WAS A MURDERER!" He shouted. "SHE KILLED HER!"

Fuck me.

"GET OUT OF HERE!" He screamed as he forced me backward on the porch.

"Wait, Sir…"

It was my worst nightmare come true. I hadn't even told England.

I needed to be the one to tell her.

"SHE KILLED ELISE!"

"IT WASN'T HER FAULT!" I screamed back.

"DAD! What's going on?" England's voice came from behind him.

"England. Please. Let me explain." I tried to call out to her from the steps of the porch. Her father just kept coming towards me, forcing me further away.

"DAD!" She yelled again. "What the hell is going on?"

I could see everything crumbling right before me. Everything was about to be shattered and there wasn't a damn thing I could do about it. Every time I tried to open my mouth to say something, her Dad would tell me to shut up.

"It was his mother who drove the car that night. It was his mother that crossed that yellow line and killed your sister. His mother is a murderer." Her Dad's voice was filled with venom. He truly believed my mom was a murdered. She wasn't. It was an accident. She just worked a twelve-hour shift. She was tired, and fell asleep.

And that was it. That was my horrible secret, and the one that completely ruined everything.

The look in England's eyes was more than I could stand to see. It was hurt, and pain. It was a look that I'd never be able to come back from. She hated me. I could see it.

I had to look away.

"LEAVE!" Her Dad screamed again.

There was nothing I could do to fix the damage that he'd done. I couldn't even turn back around to look at her before I left. Instead, I just climbed in my car and peeled out of there as fast as I could, leaving England alone there with those awful people. She was hurt and I caused it, and instead of being able to comfort her like I needed to, I left her. They wouldn't take care of her. They wouldn't make sure that she had a shoulder to cry on. Those two didn't give a damn if she was okay or not.

I pulled the car over and slammed my palm down hard onto the steering wheel.

This was the biggest mistake of my life. I loved England more than anything, and I never wanted to be the person who caused her pain. Her Dad was wrong. I should've been the one to tell her.

Why did I wait? Why didn't I tell her when I had the chance?

23

England

I couldn't talk to anyone for the rest of the night. My mind was in such a fog. The look on my Dad's face never changed. He was so angry. He was angrier than I'd ever seen him. I thought he was going to kill Will right there on our front porch. His words were vile and if Will had been closer to him, my Dad probably would have strangled him with his bare hands.

I kept replaying the words over and over in my mind. Each time, I wondered how Will so easily kept this information from me. It was like it was no big deal. Hearing my Dad say it hit me like an exploding grenade, and all I wanted to do was shut myself up in my bedroom and away from the world.

There was no way to express all the emotions I was feeling, so I chose to sleep instead. I took one of my sleeping pills, curled up in a fetal position on my bed, and drifted off.

By three a.m. I was up, and the feeling was no different. It was worse actually. Not only was I an emotional wreck, I also felt like I had a hangover. My head was pounding, my shoulder was aching, and I felt like I could toss my cookies at any given second.

Coffee... I needed coffee.

Everything downstairs was quiet and dark. I tiptoed through the kitchen and rummaged through the cabinets. I needed coffee and an aspirin in pronto fashion.

I had just sat down on the couch when the sound of footsteps came down the hall. Looking over my shoulder, I saw my Mom. She was wearing her morning robe and had her long hair pulled back in a bun. She'd been awake for a while. I could tell because there wasn't a hair out of place. Maybe she hadn't been to sleep at all.

She peeked around the corner at me and offered a small smile. It was weird, like some other kind of planet weird. Had we moved on that quickly to the point that she could stand to be around me? Did I mention it was weird?

I took another sip of my coffee and tucked my legs up under me when she came in to sit down.

She sat down on the couch.

She sat down on the couch right next to me.

There we were, sitting together on the couch. Neither of us moved. We just stared straight ahead in silence. It was completely unnatural.

One of us had to break the silence, and I waited impatiently for her to be the one. She had to be the one. I'd spoken first the day before. I couldn't put myself out there two days in a row. Especially considering how I felt. My emotions were all over the place, and I was feeling like the one person in the world who loved me had just betrayed me in the worst way.

The minutes passed, and I could feel myself tearing up. Every thought went straight back to Will. I'd given him all I had to give, and he crumbled me up like an old newspaper. How could he do that to me?

I looked far away from my Mom when the tears started to roll down my cheeks. I was trying to hide them. I didn't want her to know, because she didn't deserve to know. Not yet anyway. We had one conversation, and while I knew it was a step in the right direction it was only a baby step. We had miles to go before we were going to get back to the way things were, if we ever could.

With my free hand, I very smoothly wiped the tears from my face.

"Do you want to talk about it?" Her voice was barely audible, but I knew she was extending me an olive branch. If I didn't take it, we'd be taking a step back instead of forward.

But before I could answer she asked a question that took me by surprise.

"Do you love him?"

"How do you..."

"I am your Mother, despite what we've been through these past few months. I've known you your entire life." She explained before lifting the coffee mug to her lips. "I also know what love looks like."

"I didn't know. I swear. I didn't know that his Mom was driving the car." I choked on my words. "And I do love him. I can't help it. I'm so mad at him, but I still love him."

It was time for her to yell at me, to tell me how stupid I was for loving him. But her reaction wasn't what I expected. "It's your life England. You're a grown up now."

I just stared at her. She could've been suffering from lack of sleep. I wasn't sure. Or maybe she took some kind of chill pill. Either way, I couldn't believe the words that were coming out of her mouth. She sounded like my Mom.

"You have to make decisions that are best for your life." She snickered.

I frowned in confusion. "What's so funny?"

She shook her head. "I remember telling your sister the same thing. We were discussing colleges, instead of boys, but I told her she had to make the best decision for her."

That made me smile. It was the first good thing I'd heard about my sister in a long time. Just weeks ago I wouldn't have been able to hear her name.

"She would've been a great journalist," I admitted. "She was so smart, much smarter than me. I wanted her to be great."

"Me too." Mom leaned her head over onto my shoulder.

Her body shook, as she cried. She was crying on my shoulder, and I couldn't let her cry alone. The two of us held each other as we grieved. Together. It was much needed and it surprisingly made me feel better.

"Have you been to her grave?" I asked Mom.

She shook her head yes. "I've been a few times," she replied.

"Would you take me?" I paused. "Today."

"Yeah," she patted my knee. "I will." She smiled. "What will you do about Will?"

I groaned. "I don't know. Dad hates him. I'm still really pissed about what he did, but I think I need to talk to him. I just need a couple of days to clear my head. I want to hear what he has to say. I don't blame him for Elise's death. I don't even think I blame his Mom, which is weird. After what Dad said, I feel like I should. But I don't. I'm just angry because he didn't tell me."

"I understand. I think talking to him would be good."

"Dad hates him." I glared at her through my thick lashes.

She snorted. "Your Dad hates the mailman. It'll be okay. He does love you though, no matter how he acts. I know that for sure."

I nodded, although I didn't quite believe her. He had a funny way of showing his love if he did. "Will has been good for me. Because of him, I've conquered so many ordinary life challenges like riding in a car. I think I was just disappointed in him more than anything. I was upset that someone I trusted didn't

213

trust me enough to tell me the truth. Does that make sense?"

"It does."

I released a deep breath. "Good, because I thought I might be going crazy."

She smiled. "It's okay to feel crazy. Love does that to you."

I don't know what came over me, but I just sort of attacked her. I was overcome with joy at having my crazy Mother back, so I just tackle hugged her on the couch.

And she hugged me back.

Call it miraculous or un-certifiable. Whatever it was, I took it. I was overjoyed to have her back. So what if we missed out on the last few months. A girl needs her mother. I could easily forgive her. I already lost my sister, and I didn't want to lose my Mom too. Not if I could help it.

After our long talk, I went upstairs to check my phone. I had this crazy premonition that there would be some missed calls or texts, and I was right. Will texted me three times to tell me he was sorry, and two more times to tell me to please call him so that we could talk.

I texted him back, and told him to give me a little time.

I just needed time, and I needed to visit my sister.

24

Will

"You don't need another drink, man," Daniel reached for my glass and managed to swipe it away from me. He's lucky I wasn't seeing straight, or else I'd choke slam him. "She'll call. Just give her time. Didn't she say she needed time?"

His face was really pissing me off, all three of them.

I came over to his place to tell him what was going on and to drink a few beers. Now all of a sudden he's all-knowing, and I'm some loose wit that's unworthy of her. Sheesh. You'd think this man was some love doctor. Melody was his first serious girlfriend and he already proposed to her. He wasn't

216

capable of giving advice. It's not what I was there for anyway. I wanted to talk to my best friend, which we were doing fine six beers ago.

My head was spinning.

Hell, the whole room was spinning.

"Come on, let's get you to bed." Daniel reached for my arm, but I pulled it away.

"I'm fine," I snapped.

The sun was starting to come up. I could see the beams shining through the living room window of Daniel's apartment. Maybe it had been long enough.

I grabbed my phone from my jeans pocket, and it was then that I learned just how drunk was too drunk to text. I couldn't see the buttons on the phone. It all looked like a big blur. One blurry screen mixed with my unstable fingers wasn't a good mix. It made me feel sicker.

Tossing the phone onto to my lap, I closed my eyes. The spinning room was still spinning under my eyelids. I wasn't sure how that was possible, but it was happening.

"Bathroom," I said as my stomach started jumping.

I felt Daniel's arm under mine as he practically lifted me up. It wasn't until several hours later that I realized we actually made it to the bathroom. I knew because that was where I woke up. My cheek was frozen to the cold tile floor and the royal thrown was the first thing I saw when my eyes cracked open. Oh, and it was not a good sight.

This was bad, and something smelled awful. A couple of whiffs and I realized the stink was me. I took self-loathing to a whole new level, and it was going to take more than a shower to make it go away.

The night was blurry after I got sick, but it must've been bad because my stomach muscles were sore. It felt like I'd done a hundred sit-ups or like someone sucker punched me a few dozen times. It was well deserved though. I was such an ass.

I sighed as I climbed up from Daniel's bathroom floor. My knees made a crunching sound as they straightened out from the bend. Under normal circumstances, I'd stagger out to my car and go home after a night like that, but I couldn't go home. My home was a hotel room, and it would feel sad and empty without England there.

I had it so bad. The lovesick, I'm a douche, tight-leashed blues. It was pathetic, but I didn't care. The only thing on my mind was England. All the worrying made me crazy, and I just wanted her back in my arms where she belonged. Every time I thought about her alone in her bedroom, unable to talk to anyone or even sleep, I wanted to break something. They didn't make idiots bigger than me.

And that man...

Her father was the biggest asshole on the planet. He didn't deserve to have her love. No wonder she wanted out of that house. Sure losing a daughter had to be the hardest thing in the world, but I lost my Mom too. My Mom didn't murder Elise. She was the most wonderful woman in the whole world, and it was a horrific accident. One that we would all have to live with for the rest of our lives. There were no murderous intentions, only sad circumstances that I wished had never happened.

"You alive in there?" Daniel knocked from the hallway outside the door.

"I think so," I squinted my eyes. Funny how noise hurts your eyes when you have a hangover, or maybe I was still drunk. Reaching for the knob, I slowly opened the door. Daniel smiled from the other side. It was a cheesy grin that hurt to look at. He was annoyingly cute, and I hated that about him.

"Good morning beautiful," he said in a chipper voice.

All I could do was stand there, glaring at him. I would not crack a smile, so help me.

"There is nothing good about this morning Snow White. Take your bird songs somewhere else."

Daniel laughed at my reference before whistling as he walked out.

"You're annoying," I called out as I followed him down the hallway into the living room.

"And cute." He popped out his hip.

I rolled my eyes. "It's too early for your madness. Where's your fiancée? Can't she keep you on a leash or something?"

220

"She had some kind of luncheon to go to, and my dress was at the dry-cleaners."

"Okay, stop." I laughed and it hurt like Hell. "I need some aspirin and caffeine. You got any?"

He walked off to the kitchen. "I've got some kind of vanilla coffee or a soda."

"Soda," I answered sitting down on the couch.

"What're your plans for the day?" He asked as he passed me the can and medicine bottle.

Popping it open, I took two of the pills before I replied. "England and I were supposed to go apartment hunting, but I guess I'll be doing that on my own. I don't know the first thing about looking for a place. It was supposed to be her that picked out what she wanted and I would get it. Isn't that how it works?"

"Pretty much," he countered. "I don't have plans today, so I'll go with you." He offered, and I accepted. I needed someone's help. I was going to take it where I could get it.

"Should we pick your dress up from the cleaners first?" I asked him seriously, and caught a very large throw pillow in my temple. Guess the joke was over.

I couldn't stop laughing, though.

25

England

After a long morning, Mom drove me across town to the graveyard so that I could see Elise's grave. It was an awful drive. Nothing like when I rode with Will. I was almost into a full-blown panic attack before were even parked. My palms were sweaty, and I could barely muster a word. Not to mention the motion sickness. I had to glare down at my feet the entire time. Everything was just easier with Will. There was no way to explain why. It just was.

Once Mom put the car in park and my hands quit shaking, I got out quickly. The cool air felt nice against my warm face, but it made my shoulder ache. I wouldn't complain, though. The ache was part of my punishment for living, the same with my hearing aids.

With my nerves being all over the place, I kept my head down. The thought of seeing her eternal resting place made my stomach turn. It was my first time being there, and I wasn't sure how I'd handle it, or even if I could.

I matched Mom's footsteps as we made our way around the soft grass, finally coming to a stop in the back near the fence.

"This is it," Mom said.

I glanced up once, and back down again not giving myself enough time to even see it. Elise and I had this special, unspeakable bond that not even my parents could understand. So I knew that I wanted to be there alone, at least for the first time.

"Can you give me a few minutes?" I asked.

"Sure," she patted my shoulder before walking away.

I took a few deep breaths before looking up again.

It was beautiful. So beautiful that it took my breath away. The stone was square, but there were the most realistic butterflies etched along the sides. They brought tears to my eyes. Elise would've loved them. It would've been exactly what she wanted. Being the girl that dressed as a butterfly for Halloween three years in a row, it was perfect.

I walked around to get a closer look.

The stone read:

Elise Noelle Murphy

Loving Daughter and Twin Sister

December 8, 1996 – July 11, 2015

The tears fell harder and wouldn't stop. I missed her so much.

So, so much…

She was my best friend.

In the time after she passed, I thought every day about the punishment of her death. I thought about how life was my punishment and how I didn't deserve happiness or even love. The thoughts consumed my every waking moment. Never once did I give thought to how Elise would feel if she were the one to have lived. Despite our faces being an exact replica of one another, our minds were different. She would've been strong enough to face the world without me. It would've hurt her, but she was tough. Not like me. I couldn't bear to face the world or myself.

I guess it takes moments like these, to wake you up. I needed absolution, my freedom from this punishment. Elise was my absolution.

I draped my arms over the headstone and cried. I cried so hard that I could barely see. If Elise had been there in that moment she would have said, "what took you so long?"

My laughter sounded out through my tears.

"I don't know, sis. Guess it wasn't really my hearing that was gone, more like my vision. I'm a big fool." I cried some more. "I'm sorry I didn't come sooner, but I promise to come visit a lot now. I'm not going to let you down. I'll get better. You wait and see. It's the hardest thing in the world not seeing your face every day. I miss you." I sobbed. "I miss you so much. It's not fair."

All this time, I was letting Elise down by not living my life. She would've wanted me to go on, just like I would've wanted her to.

"Feeling better," my Mom's still annoying voice rang from behind me and my hearing aid started to make that beeping noise again. The battery had to be changed soon.

"A little," I admitted. "I'm glad I came."

"Me too. What do you say about me making dinner tonight? I think it would be a good time for you to talk to your Dad, and maybe get some things off your chest. I'll talk to him beforehand so maybe it won't be so bad?"

My shoulders sagged. Talking to my Dad sounded like a lost cause. He was never going to understand my reasoning for loving Will, and he was never going to be okay with it. "I don't know," I shook my head.

In my mind, a voice said, "Give him a chance."

227

I looked back at the headstone. Elise was Daddy's girl so I knew that voice must've been hers. I smiled, and rubbed my hand over the stone once more.

"Okay." I agreed.

"Good, let's go."

Walking along the grassy pathway, I noticed just off to the right the word "Edmunds" on the back of a headstone.

Could it be?

"Just a second," I called out to Mom.

Walking around to the other side of the stone I read the name allowed. "Gloria Anne Edmunds."

I didn't know Will's Mothers name, but looking at the dates confirmed my suspicions. The date of death was July 11, 2015.

"It's Will's Mom."

She had a pretty headstone with a little dove on the front, and the words "loving mother" were etched on it. There were no flowers so I wasn't sure if Will ever visited. Maybe it was too hard for him.

I looked up at Mom to see a sad look on her face.

"Can I give her one of Elise's flowers? She has so many."

Mom nodded. "Absolutely." I was thankful that at least one of my parents was seeing clearly. Mom was aware that it was an accident no matter how bad it hurt.

I pulled a few daisies from Elise's bouquet and placed them in front of Gloria's grave.

"Rest in peace, Gloria. Elise would be happy to share her flowers with you."

***

Before I sat down for what was sure to be the dinner theatre, I texted Will. I asked him if he'd pick me up after dinner so we could talk. Truthfully, I just didn't want to spend another sleepless night away from him. He texted me quickly saying he'd be over around eight o'clock, but that he wasn't coming to the door. Who could blame him?

The three of us, my Mom, Dad, and me sat down around the dinner table. It was the first time in months that we'd shared a family meal. Honestly, I couldn't remember the last time.

Mom had obviously prepared Dad because he looked up from his plate at least twice. It was like some miracle or something.

I kept thinking about the voice in my head telling me to give him a chance, but I could also hear the bell ringing for round one.

Mom spoke first. I suppose she was trying to break the ice. My guess was that it was nearly six inches thick, and that she'd need an axe to get through it.

"We all need to talk about the plans we have for the next few weeks." Mom suggested.

This wasn't going to end well. I could feel it in my bones.

"We're moving. What other kinds of plans could there be?" Dad was Mr. Blunt with his words. He always was the man of few words.

Mom, looked at me with commanding eyes like she wanted me to step in and say something. I couldn't take the immense pressure, which was unfortunate. Because once I got the nerve up to open my mouth, I skipped round one and went straight for the knockout. Obviously, I got my lack of words from my Dad.

"I'm moving in with Will," I blurted out as I shoveled in another bite of mashed potatoes.

"Like hell you are?"

"Richard!" my Mom barked.

I knew he wouldn't be keen on the whole idea. Actually, I was prepared for it. His words didn't faze me. I just continued to eat as if he'd never spoken. I loved my Dad, but I was old enough to make my own decisions, and I'd already made my mind up. So long as Will would still have me. I could only hope.

"How could you do this to your sister?" My Dad lectured.

"No! No, no, no, no, no." I shook my head. "You're not going to try and make me feel guilty for this. I'm sorry, but you're not. I'm finally getting better. I'm finally making peace with this horrible reality, and I'm not going to let you do this to me. She's my sister, and I love her more than anything. I get that you're mad, and sad, and whatever else. But he played no part in what happened to her."

Dad's face was as red as I'd ever seen it. Like he could ransack the whole house and not think twice about it. "It was his Mother."

"It was an accident, Richard." My Mom tried to reason with him. "We can't hold someone responsible, especially when that someone lost her life too. There is nobody to blame. It was an accident."

"I can blame who I want." He said, sounding like a two-year-old child.

"Dad."

"Richard." My mom rested her hand on his. "I'm mad too. I've blamed everybody for this, including myself. But I realize now that I can't blame anyone because it was an accident. Don't blame that boy. England loves him."

My Dad snapped his head back to me, and suddenly I felt like a tiny little girl about to be scolded by her Father. Mom's words just spewed out. Maybe it was a family trait.

There were tears in his eyes, and it hurt me. I would never want to disappoint him in any way, and I had a feeling he was about to walk out of my life and never look back. I was afraid that I would lose him for good. That wasn't what I wanted.

He looked at me harder than he ever had. I felt like he was looking for something, like answers. It was intense, and within seconds it was gone. He stood up from the table with force and stomped off towards his bedroom. He never said another word.

I couldn't sit at that table for another minute, so I followed his cue. I stood up and walked straight to the front door. Mom yelled after me, but I didn't stop. I needed Will.

26

Will

There she was standing on her porch waiting for me the moment I pulled up. Dammit I missed her, and I wanted to run to her a scoop her and up in my arms. The only problem was I didn't know how pissed she was at me. This talk could be the one where she'd tell me it wasn't going to happen.

I waited for her move, and she was moving quickly.

She was running.

Shit.

I climbed out the car to meet her. Something was wrong.

"England."

She ran right to me and wrapped her arms around my neck.

"Baby, are you okay?" I squeezed her waist and pulled her as close to me as I could get her.

She smelled amazing. I missed that smell. Her face was buried in my neck, and I realized that maybe she couldn't hear me. I wasn't thinking when I spoke. I didn't look to see if her hearing aids were in.

"Baby!" I yelled.

"Don't yell," she answered. "I'm fine. I just need you. I need you to hold me."

"Oh," I moaned. "I needed to hear that baby. I'm so sorry for…"

Her lips crashed hard into mine making my knees week. If we weren't sitting in her parent's driveway then I'd take her right there on the hood of my car.

"Take me away from here." She begged.

"Get in."

I knew just where I wanted to take her.

When we pulled up at the house, she gave me a weird look. I was expecting her too. She had no idea what I'd been up to since she was gone.

"Where are we Will?" She asked.

I smiled. "Come on. I want to show you something."

She cocked her head to the side, but followed my lead. I led us up the walkway and up to the front door. I slid the key in the lock and opened the door. Standing there, I motioned for her to go in first.

I waited until she had stepped onto the hardwood floor of the foyer before I switched on the light. She covered her mouth with her hand, and her eyes grew wide.

"How did you do this?" She continued shaking her head.

I wrapped an arm loosely around her shoulder. "Well. Daniel and I went on an apartment hunt today, and after looking at two places I knew we needed a house instead. I kept trying to think, about what you'd like but I realized I had no idea." I laughed. It was the truth because I really didn't know that much about her, but I remembered plenty of things she didn't like. "When the realtor showed me this place, I loved it. I kept thinking that you'd love it too, or I hoped you would. Truthfully, I pictured you naked in every room."

"WILL!" She smacked my arm.

At least she didn't hit my nose.

"A man can dream." I winked. "Anyway, the realtor said the owners were wanting to do a quick sale, because they're leaving the country. So with my large cash down payment, they handed over the keys. I sign the paperwork tomorrow."

"I can't believe we're doing this. I just can't believe it. You bought a house."

"We bought a house," I corrected.

"We barely know each other."

"When you know, you know," I replied with a grin, and I believed it. "Come on, look around. Tell me what you think? I hope you like it."

She kept shaking her head in disbelief. "I love it."

"But you haven't even walked inside. Come on."

"I don't have to walk inside. If you love it, I love it," she admitted.

I claimed her lips with mine and took her hand. I couldn't wait for her to see the rest.

"Wow!" She said in every room.

There were three bedrooms, two bathrooms, an office, and an extra large kitchen. The backyard had the most amazing view, and a wood fence just like the one at her house. I could picture her sitting out there next to it every night.

I turned on the back porch light, and the two of us sat down on the wooden swing. She snuggled into my side and tucked her feet up next to her.

"We need to talk about what happened?" I suggested. Not because I wanted to. The idea of it gave me a tension headache, but it needed to be done. We couldn't just pretend that nothing happened.

She rolled her head over so that she was facing me. "We don't have to talk about it."

"I think we do. I want to tell you what happened. I don't want you to think that my Mom is a murderer."

"I don't," she placed her hand on my chest.

"Please. Let me finish. My Mom worked a double shift that night at the factory. She wasn't even supposed to be working at all, but they were on some kind of mandatory overtime. She called me on her last break to tell me that she'd be home in a couple of hours, so I waited up for her. When she worked late I liked to fix us something to eat, because she was always so tired. The policeman that night said she crossed over the yellow line. She wasn't texting. I know because she said it took too long, that she'd rather call people. So they came to the conclusion that she probably fell asleep at the wheel. I didn't request an autopsy to tell me any differently. I mean maybe she could've had a heart attack, but she worked a double shift. I'm sure she fell asleep.

"I was going to tell you. I promise I was, but I was scared. You were still grieving and dealing with your own problems. I didn't think it would be right to pile on more."

"I understand Will. I promise. I needed time to think about what happened, so I could clear my head.

I'm glad I did too. My Mom and I really got to talk, and she is so much better now. We even went to see my sister's grave." England smiled.

I kissed her perky lips. "That's great."

"My Dad and I might never speak again, but I got my Mom back. Oh, and I saw your Mom's grave too."

"You did?"

"Yes. I even gave her some of my sister's daisies."

Wow. I glanced up at the clouds trying to hold myself together. There were so many times that I wanted to go and visit her grave but I couldn't. The last time I was there was the day she was buried.

"You're incredible." I stood up from the swing taking her with me. "I love you."

"I love you too." Her hands rested on my shoulders and she tiptoed up to me for a kiss. "Now, don't fight with me again or I'll break your nose."

I covered my nose quickly and very nasally said, "Leave the nose alone."

"Take me to our bedroom William Edmunds."

I lifted her up off her feet. "We don't have a bed yet."

"We don't need a bed."

27

England

A week had passed since we'd closed on the house, and things were going pretty good, except I still hadn't talked to my Dad. Every time I called the house, he'd say "hold on" and put my Mom on the phone. He was a barrel of fun, and I'd grown used to the idea that he just wasn't going to break. Maybe one day, but it was going to take him some time. There was nothing I could do to change that.

Mom said that they were leaving on Saturday, which was only five days away. She wanted me to come by before then and get the furniture I wanted. They were going to buy new and she said I could have what I wanted from the house. Mostly, I wanted a few of Elise's things, and we didn't have a kitchen table yet, so I wanted that too.

Will found a job working part-time at a local packaging company, and he seemed to really like it or at least the people he worked with. He only took part-time hours because he said he was ready to go back to school. My man and his ambitions, sigh…

The two of us had found ourselves a routine that worked for us, and mine mostly consisted of one day out of the house a week. I was okay with being a hermit, but Will said that would change. He thought I was getting better every day, which I was, but I'd grown used to the idea of being a homebody and it worked for me.

So despite our newly found flaws, things were going great. I was getting used to Will's obsession with all things sports, and he could name most of the girls on *The Real Housewives.*

The only thing missing he says, it that I haven't met his friends. That situation was being rectified with dinner and football at our new place. We were only two hours away from them showing up, and I felt like I could use a very large anxiety pill. It meant so much to Will for me to meet them that I wouldn't dare tell him that. Instead, I just sucked it up. A few hours with the people he loved most couldn't be that bad. Right?

"You look hot, babe," he came up from behind me and placed his arms around my stomach. "Are you wearing makeup?"

I glanced at him from over my shoulder. "Just mascara."

He'd never seen me with makeup. I didn't bother with it because it meant looking in the mirror. Since my reflection didn't scare me anymore, I thought it couldn't hurt to make an effort.

"You don't need it, you know?"

"I don't need boobs either," I countered.

"I retract my last statement."

I patted his cheek. "Good thinking."

There was a knock on the door and I gave Will the I'm-scared look, and he kissed my lips. "Don't worry okay? They'll love you."

"I'm not worried about them loving me, I just don't do well with conversation. Hermit, remember?"

"Come on my gorgeous hermit." He took my hand and led me to the living room. I shuffled my feet and waited nervously as he opened the door. A young couple stood on the other side, and I assumed it was Daniel and Melody. He had short, sandy brown hair, and she was a leggy blonde. They were a sickeningly beautiful couple.

"This is England," I heard Will say before he pulled me into his side. A half smile was the best I could do under pressure. "This is Daniel and Melody."

I lifted my hand up for an uncomfortable wave and tried to keep my face calm as I said hello.

"Where's Jace?" Will asked.

"Right here you sexy son of a bitch," a voice said from the entryway.

My smile grew. I liked Jace already.

We exchanged hellos and Will invited them to come in and hang out. We'd ordered some pizzas and bought some beers for the game. I couldn't tell you what game or which sport, but there was a ball and some players. Enough said.

"England," Melody said as she scooted closer to me on the couch. "Do you like sports?" She asked.

"No," I smirked.

"Do you have coffee?"

Thank goodness. "Yes, yes I do."

We stood up from the couch and walked to the kitchen. The guys didn't even know we left.

"I swear, sports suck. I could almost nap through it."

"I know what you mean," I replied as I started the coffee. "And there are so many. Does Daniel watch golf?" I asked her.

She grumbled. "Yes. It's the ultimate snooze fest."

I agreed. There was nothing more boring than golf.

"So, do you work?" I grabbed the coffee mugs from the cupboard.

"No," she answered. "I'm currently in college, so my parents don't want me working. My Dad expects me to take over the family business one day. Yay me," she said sarcastically.

"Bummer."

"What do you do?"

I poured our coffee. "Nothing at the moment, but there was a time when I wanted to go to college. I feel like I'd rather do an online type of thing though. I'm kind of a homebody."

"There's nothing wrong with that."

Maybe conversation wasn't as hard as I thought it was. At least I was making the effort.

"So." Her eyebrows arched.

"Soooo," I gave her a side glance.

"You and Will." She smiled. "He seems happy."

What was she getting at, because I wasn't prepared for details about us? We were just beginning to be an "us."

"He's a good guy," she explained, as if I needed convincing.

"I know. We're good." I hesitated with my words. If she wanted more detail than that she was going to have to get me drunk first, and not caffeine drunk.

"You girls okay?" Will asked when he came into the kitchen.

"We're great." Melody replied. "I was about to try and talk England into having lunch at the club with me next week. The food's great."

She caught me by surprise, and when I looked up at Will, he had a cheesy grin on his face. He desperately wanted me to make friends with her. I could see it all over his face.

"Sure," I agreed although I wasn't enthused. Don't get me wrong. Melody seemed nice and sweet, but lunch in a public place was a whole other ball game for me.

"Great!" Melody said. "We better get back in there with the guys before they start throwing food at the T.V."

I gave Will a questioning look. "It happened one time." He rolled his eyes. "She won't let us live it down."

"It was pasta," she said to me.

I had a feeling there would always be something exciting happening with this group around.

***

"So, what did you think about them? They're a bit nuts right?" Will pulled me down onto his lap.

I straddled him staring into those gorgeous eyes of his. With all the pressure of the day, I felt like I was right where I needed to be when I was that close to him.

"It'll take some time to get used to them."

"It was good. They were good." I kissed his cheek. "I liked them, so stop worrying."

"They liked you too." He softly kissed the edge of my lips.

"What's not to like?"

"Mhmm." He groaned as I shifted on his lap.

I placed my hands on either side of his neck and let my lips graze his before pressing them hard together. He was an amazing kisser. I couldn't seem to get enough of him.

His hands snaked up under my top and gripped my sides, pulling me farther down onto him. He was an aggressive man in the bedroom, and I loved it. He knew what he wanted and he wasn't afraid to tell me. To be honest, it took little persuading for me to surrender to his every move. He was just that good. There was this thing he did with his eyes that made you melt under his gaze. Damn I loved it.

I raised my arms in the air, and he lifted my shirt up over my head. Wrapping my arms around his neck, I whispered in his ear. "I want you."

That was all it took. He had us up off the couch and in the bedroom in under a minute.

I watched him as he slipped out of his loose fitting jeans. I tried to tease him and undress slowly, but he growled like a bear in frustration. He was a ravenous beast. I loved it when he did that. It made my insides scream.

I'd barely gotten my jeans off before he had bent me over the bed. My hands stretched out wide along the sheets, and my legs spread apart with ease. His teasing fingers enticed me.

He softly stroked the edge of my behind as he drove himself inside me. His thrusts were hard just the way I liked it, while his fingertips moved slow over my ass cheeks. It was the sweetest kind of pleasure.

The rocking motion left me pleading for more. When I screamed out his name, his movements grew harder and harder until my legs grew weak beneath me.

When I knew he was close to his max, I reached between my legs and moved my fingertips along the wetness until I was right there with him.

He moved rapidly until the last thrust, and I was sure my eyes rolled back into my head. Everything inside me was tingling. Right down to my toes.

There was nothing better than sex with Will.

I promise you.

Nothing was better.

28

Will

England had been upset all week because her parents were leaving. She didn't come right out and admit that was the problem, but it didn't take a genius to recognize it. The mention of their names, or anything associated clearly upset her.

I dropped her off early that morning at their house so that she could box up the things she wanted and promised I'd be back to get her. I first had to take care of a few things, and I wanted to get a few pieces of furniture from my Mom's house too.

After borrowing my friends' truck, I made the twenty-minute drive out to the edge of town where my Mom's house still sat vacant. It was exactly the way that I'd left it, other than the uncut grass that had almost grown up over the sidewalk.

I made a mental note as I walked up the steps of all the things that needed to be taken care of. It'd be a full-time job keeping up with both houses.

The thought crossed my mind that I may be able to rent Mom's house to a nice family or even sell it. England wouldn't oppose to either. She never minded my crazy antics, and always listened to me when I needed someone to talk to or confide in. It was one of her many amazing traits.

Walking through the house brought back so many memories. I considered this place my home. It was my home, for many years. But now it seemed lonely and sad. The quietness was upsetting. It just didn't seem right that the place was dark, and that I couldn't hear the radio from the kitchen, or the tea pot on the stove, or even the television from her bedroom. I hated it.

Combing my fingertips through my hair, I let out a deep breath. I came there for a reason, and it wasn't to reminisce. A job needed to be done, and I only had an hour before it'd be time to pick up England.

I grabbed a couple of plastic totes out of the garage and made my way around the house getting the things that I knew I wanted to keep, like the little mementos that meant so much to my Mom. Though I didn't want to, and I hesitated, I finally made my way inside Mom's bedroom. It was a stupid idea. I got choked up just seeing her unmade bed. The only thing I wanted out of that room was my Mom's old jewelry box. I thought maybe England would like to have it to use, otherwise I wouldn't have even went inside.

I spotted the old box on her dresser and grabbed it quickly before practically running out of the room. That was enough for the day. My stomach was in knots.

I locked the front door and pulled it closed behind me. Then I hauled ass out of there. Next time I'd take England with me. It was too depressing to be there by myself.

When I pulled up outside England's parents' house. I didn't get out. Not that I was scared to. I just knew that her Dad would be ready to pounce on me like a lion again. If he didn't hate me so much, I would've already proposed to that girl. He was the only thing standing in my way.

Sounds crazy to propose to someone you've only dated for a couple of months I know, but she was it for me.

She was the one and only girl that I'd ever need.

I couldn't ask her, though. Not while that man still hated me. Even though England said that she didn't care what he thought, I knew she really did. It mattered to her, which meant it mattered to me.

Plain and simple.

I sat there for a bit and scrolled down through my Facebook page. As usual, it was the same old boring shit, just a different day. I was about to text England to see if she was close to finishing up, when a knock on my window scared the shit out of me.

You've got to be kidding me.

Her Dad stood outside my window waiting for me to roll it down. Over and over in my mind, all I could think was that I wasn't in the mood for another fight with him. My mood was crappy already, and I wouldn't be able to listen to him call my Mother a murderer again.

Turning over the ignition, I hit the button to lower the window.

"Sir," I said in a bitter tone. Again, I wasn't in the mood.

"We need to talk." His deep voice sounded serious.

My right hand grasped the steering wheel so hard that I thought I'd break the damn thing off. "I don't think…"

"It'll only take a minute," he interrupted.

I held my tongue, but I really didn't want to.

"Fine," was all I could say.

I switched the key back off and climbed out of the car. Slipping my hands deep in my pockets, I leaned back against my car door. There was no eye contact, because it killed me to look at him. He was an arrogant man, and I don't know how in the world he had such a wonderful daughter.

256

"I'll be quick," he said. "I just wanted to say I'm sorry."

My head snapped up, and I'm pretty sure I said "what" out loud, not meaning to.

"I don't want to lose England, too," he whispered. "I realize that I needed someone to blame, and I'd already made it down the list. Your Mom was all that was left."

I swallowed roughly.

He spoke again. "She loves you, and I want her to be happy despite how horrible I seem. It's just been the hardest few months of my life. It's not easy for a man like me to admit when he's wrong, but I was wrong. I've been incredibly hard headed and the biggest pain in the ass lately. It took me all this time to realize that I still had a daughter and that if I didn't straighten up I was going to lose her too.

"Now I'm not saying that I like you. I really don't know you. But England chose you, so I guess that's saying something. All I ask of you is that you treat her right. Don't do what I did, because she deserves better. And don't ever hit her. She's my little girl, and I love her too. If you hurt her, I'll kill you."

"Yes, sir." I responded. I was still a bit stunned as I stood there in shock. "I'll…" I stuttered. "I'll take care of her. I promise."

"Good. Come on then. There's supper inside and they're waiting for us to come in and eat."

What the hell just happened?

"Come on," he waved.

29

England

I felt sort of guilty that I didn't prepare Will for the wrath of my Dad, but once I saw his face, the guilt went away. I wanted to laugh so badly. He was staring at me wide-eyed as he sat down at the dinner table. He looked like a deer that had been caught in the headlights. It was so funny. Even my Mom snickered when she saw him. The poor guy was in a state of shock like I'd never seen before. He was going to get double-whammied when I told him the other news tonight. I couldn't wait.

Dad didn't have much to say at the table, but chimed in a few times. It was more than I could've hoped for. The fact that he was even sitting at the table was more than enough for me. Not once did he say anything mean to Will. During the times when I thought he might, he'd just shovel his food in faster. Mom was great too. She made small talk about the silliest things, and it seemed to help smooth over the tense situations. All and all I'd say the dinner went well, after Will finally warmed up. It was almost like the old days, only Will was sitting in Elise's spot. She wouldn't mind, though. If she were there to see him, she'd approve.

Mom and I cleared the dishes and talked a little while longer before it was time to go. I think the two of us finally had an understanding. She wished me well and we even talked about a future visit, which sounded pretty good.

We said our goodbyes on the steps of the front porch, and I cried a little as I hugged my parents. It would be the last time that I'd be inside the house I'd grown up in, and the feelings sank in as we stood outside. I'd never get to run back up those stairs to my room, or shimmy down the side of the house to my secret spot. It seemed surreal to me.

I was having the hardest time releasing mom's hand. I'd just got my parents back, and now they were leaving me. It felt like I was being cheated, but I knew they had to go. It was best for them to get a fresh start. The same way I was.

It just hurt.

"We'll be back at Christmas for a few days, so plan on us coming for a visit," my Mom stated, and I could tell by the look on my Dad's face that he wasn't as excited about the idea. He was a one-step-at-a-time kind of man.

"I can't wait," I admitted truthfully.

I waved goodbye as Will and I got into the car and pulled away.

"You okay, Babe?" He asked.

"Yeah," I shook my head. "Could we get ice cream on the way home?"

He laughed. "How can you still be hungry? Your Mom cooked for like ten people."

"Just am," I shrugged with a smile. "Wait, pull over" I called out.

"What's wrong?" Will was concerned.

"Hurry," I said feeling my insides turning.

He hadn't even made it to a complete stop before I threw open my door, and puked. I couldn't stop. My stomach was turning like I was spinning around on an amusement ride.

"Babe, are you okay? Here, take this water." He passed the water bottle over my shoulder.

I heard the car door shut and saw him come around to my side. "You don't want to see this. Get back in the car." I called out as my head draped over between my legs.

"You're sick. I'm here for you."

"Oh," I groaned.

He rubbed my back gently.

"I hope you plan on doing this for me for the next nine months," I told him.

"Baby, I'll be here for you for the rest of your life."

Be still my thunderous heart. He was the sweetest pain in the ass ever.

"Wait," he stopped rubbing. "Nine months?"

I looked up at him through my watery eyes. He had that same stunned look on his face that he had a dinner. Too bad I wasn't feeling good enough to snap a picture. I could laugh at that face for years to come.

"Deep breaths, Daddy. It'll be okay."

"Daddy," he repeated the words, but it came out more like a mumble. It was cute.

"Yep." I used my sleeve to wipe my face and slid my feet back into the car. "Now take me for ice cream."

Closing the door, I waited for him to climb back in the car but the door never opened. When I looked out the window, he was still standing there with that stunned look on his face. So, I took advantage. I opened the car door and snapped a picture on my phone. That one was going in the baby book.

"Will! Ice Cream!"

"Right," he ran around the car in a panic and climbed back behind the wheel. "I can't believe it," he said.

"Well, you've got several months to get used to the idea."

He smiled the biggest smile. "I love you so much, England."

"I love you too, Will."

Epilogue

England

The spring season was in full bloom, and Elise's grave was covered with the most beautiful daisies. Those were her favorite flowers, so I kept the ground covered in them. I also shared them with Gloria.

Will still never visited the graveyard with me, so I made sure I stopped and talked to his Mom every time I was there. Just to tell her that he was good and that he missed her. Lately, I'd been coming a lot. With only twelve weeks left until the twins arrived, I was becoming more and more emotional. It didn't help that I hadn't seen my feet in weeks.

This would be the last time that I got to visit Elise before the babies came, because Will was the most overprotective husband that anyone could ever have. It was a fight just to leave the house.

After getting my big booty on the ground, I was realizing his concerns. It was going to take a bulldozer to get me back up.

I made myself as comfortable as I could before I started my talk. Thank goodness I remembered my tissues because the last time was a water work disaster.

"Hey, Sis. I made it back this week. Barely. Will was fuming mad because I left the house, so I can't stay long. It's going to be a while before I get to come back. The doctor thinks Riley and Reagan will be making an early appearance. I guess it's a girl thing. At least that's what Will says. I still can't believe we're having twins." I shook my head. "Mom says its fate. She truly believes that you have something to do with it. Gosh, you should see her. She's like the energizer grandmother. You'd be impressed. Anyway, I was sitting in the nursery yesterday and thinking about you. Well us. And I thought about how the two of us always had the greatest bond. How we were so inseparable as kids. I hope that my girls are the same way. I hope they're best friends, and that they never have to go through what we did. I tried to talk to Will about how I was feeling, but he just didn't understand. Not the way that you would. I'm a little scared. Actually, I'm a lot scared. I'm afraid that one day they'll be separated like us."

Bring on the tears.

"I'm crazy. I know. I just can't get a grasp on reality, and I think my hormones make it a thousand times worse. Once I see their beautiful faces, I'm sure I'll feel differently. I can't wait to see those faces. Let's hope I don't mix them up. Could you imagine what Mom would say to that?" I laughed. "I remember there was a time when I hated sharing a face with you. Boy, was I stupid. It's a special bond that I'll always only have with you, and my girls will get to have it, too. That makes me happy. Well, I guess I better go now before Will sends out the search and rescue team. I love you, Elise. I'll bring the girls to see you as soon as I can, and I'll give them lots of kisses for you. Wish me luck, Sis."

Before leaving I grabbed some daisies from Elise's grave and placed them on Gloria's just beside the newly etched words –Loving Grandma.

Acknowledgments

I'd like to thank my family first. My husband Jason and my kids were so supportive during the writing process of this book. They let me write on days when I should've been doing family things, and they understood that my laptop needed to be open while we watched movies. They really love me. And I love them all so much, and wouldn't be where I am today without them.

A big thank you to my best friend Micalea, who truly helped me more than she'll ever know. When I thought I was going to pull my hair out, she was there. When I got frustrated and wanted to toss my laptop out the window, she was there. When I wanted to cry and cuss, she was there. I love you Micalea, and without you I'd be lost.

How about that cover?? Gorgeous right?? Thank you so much Emily Wittig for designing this beautiful cover. It couldn't be more fitting for England's story. You're a rock star, my love.

To my beta readers Raquel and Shelby... I don't know what I'd do without you. Thank you for your time, effort, and support. Thank you for letting me send things to you just days before release. You don't know how much you mean to me.

Thank you so much to the book-lovers out there. Thanks for taking a chance on my books, and sharing them with the world once you do. You're the greatest, and I know I wouldn't be where I am without your love and support. Keep reading!! Knowledge is power!!

About The Author

Regina is a contemporary romance writer from Kentucky. She lives there with her husband and her two kids. She can be found behind her computer, a good book, or watching sports. She loves to hear from her readers. You can find out what's coming next if you follow her on Facebook at https://www.facebook.com/AuthReginaBartley/

To keep up with all things book-related from Author Regina Bartley you could sign up to receive her newsletter here → https://goo.gl/zXYnLC

63346517R00153

Made in the USA
Charleston, SC
02 November 2016